This Is How You Lose Her

FICTION

JUNOT DÍAZ

RIVERHEAD BOOKS   *a member of Penguin Group (USA) Inc.*   *New York* 2012

This
Is
How
You
Lose
Her

RIVERHEAD BOOKS
Published by the Penguin Group
Penguin Group (USA) Inc., 375 Hudson Street, New York, New York 10014,
USA • Penguin Group (Canada), 90 Eglinton Avenue East, Suite 700, Toronto,
Ontario M4P 2Y3, Canada (a division of Pearson Penguin Canada Inc.) • Penguin
Books Ltd, 80 Strand, London WC2R 0RL, England • Penguin Ireland, 25 St
Stephen's Green, Dublin 2, Ireland (a division of Penguin Books Ltd) • Penguin
Group (Australia), 250 Camberwell Road, Camberwell, Victoria 3124, Australia
(a division of Pearson Australia Group Pty Ltd) • Penguin Books India Pvt Ltd,
11 Community Centre, Panchsheel Park, New Delhi–110 017, India • Penguin
Group (NZ), 67 Apollo Drive, Rosedale, North Shore 0632, New Zealand (a division of Pearson New Zealand Ltd) • Penguin Books (South Africa) (Pty) Ltd,
24 Sturdee Avenue, Rosebank, Johannesburg 2196, South Africa

Penguin Books Ltd, Registered Offices: 80 Strand, London WC2R 0RL, England

Grateful acknowledgment is made to reprint an excerpt from *My Wicked Wicked
Ways*. Copyright © 1987 by Sandra Cisneros. Published by Third Woman Press and
in hardcover by Alfred A. Knopf. By permission of Third Woman Press and Susan
Bergholz Literary Services, New York, New York, and Lamy, New Mexico. All
rights reserved.

The following stories have been previously published, in a slightly different form: in
The New Yorker, "The Sun, the Moon, the Stars," "Otravida, Otravez," "The Pura
Principle," "Alma," and "Nilda"; in *Glimmer Train*, "Invierno"; and in *Story*, "Flaca."

ISBN 978-1-59448-642-5

Printed in the United States of America

BOOK DESIGN BY NICOLE LAROCHE

This is a work of fiction. Names, characters, places, and incidents either are the
product of the author's imagination or are used fictitiously, and any resemblance to
actual persons, living or dead, businesses, companies, events, or locales is entirely
coincidental.

For Marilyn Ducksworth and Mih-Ho Cha
in honor of your friendship, your fierceness, your grace

The Sun, the Moon, the Stars   1

Nilda   27

Alma   43

Otravida, Otravez   49

Flaca   77

The Pura Principle   89

Invierno   119

Miss Lora   147

The Cheater's Guide to Love   173

Okay, we didn't work, and all
memories to tell you the truth aren't good.
But sometimes there were good times.
Love was good. I loved your crooked sleep
beside me and never dreamed afraid.

There should be stars for great wars
like ours.

SANDRA CISNEROS

The Sun, the Moon, the Stars

I'M NOT A BAD GUY. I know how that sounds—defensive, unscrupulous—but it's true. I'm like everybody else: weak, full of mistakes, but basically good. Magdalena disagrees though. She considers me a typical Dominican man: a sucio, an asshole. See, many months ago, when Magda was still my girl, when I didn't have to be careful about almost anything, I cheated on her with this chick who had tons of eighties freestyle hair. Didn't tell Magda about it, either. You know how it is. A smelly bone like that, better off buried in the backyard of your life. Magda only found out because homegirl wrote her a fucking *letter*. And the letter had *details*. Shit you wouldn't even tell your boys drunk.

The thing is, that particular bit of stupidity had been over for months. Me and Magda were on an upswing. We weren't as distant as we'd been the winter I was cheating. The freeze was over. She was coming over to my place and instead of us hanging with my knucklehead boys—me smoking, her bored out of her skull—we were seeing movies. Driving out to different places to eat. Even caught a play at the Crossroads and I took her picture with some bigwig black playwrights, pictures where she's smiling so much you'd think her wide-ass mouth was going to unhinge. We were a couple again. Visiting each other's family on the weekends. Eating breakfast at diners hours before anybody else was up, rummaging through the New Brunswick library together, the one Carnegie built with his guilt money. A nice rhythm we had going. But then the Letter hits like a *Star Trek* grenade and detonates everything, past, present, future. Suddenly her folks want to kill me. It don't matter that I helped them with their taxes two years running or that I mow their lawn. Her father, who used to treat me like his hijo, calls me an asshole on the phone, sounds like he's strangling himself with the cord. You no deserve I speak to you in Spanish, he says. I see one of Magda's girlfriends at the Woodbridge mall—Claribel, the ecuatoriana with the biology degree and the chinita eyes—and she treats me like I ate somebody's favorite kid.

You don't even want to hear how it went down with Magda. Like a five-train collision. She threw Cassandra's letter at me—it missed and landed under a Volvo—and then she sat down on the curb and started hyperventilating. Oh, God, she wailed. Oh, my God.

This is when my boys claim they would have pulled a Total Fucking Denial. Cassandra *who*? I was too sick to my stomach even to try. I sat down next to her, grabbed her flailing arms, and said some dumb shit like You have to listen to me, Magda. Or you won't understand.

LET ME TELL YOU about Magda. She's a Bergenline original: short with a big mouth and big hips and dark curly hair you could lose a hand in. Her father's a baker, her mother sells kids' clothes door to door. She might be nobody's pendeja but she's also a forgiving soul. A Catholic. Dragged me into church every Sunday for Spanish Mass, and when one of her relatives is sick, especially the ones in Cuba, she writes letters to some nuns in Pennsylvania, asks the sisters to pray for her family. She's the nerd every librarian in town knows, a teacher whose students love her. Always cutting shit out for me from the newspapers, Dominican shit. I see her like, what, every week, and she still sends me corny little notes in the mail: So you won't forget me. You couldn't think of anybody worse to screw than Magda.

Anyway I won't bore you with what happens after she finds out. The begging, the crawling over glass, the crying. Let's just say that after two weeks of this, of my driving out to her house, sending her letters, and calling her at all hours of the night, we put it back together. Didn't mean I ever ate with her family again or that her girlfriends were celebrating. Those cabronas, they were like, No, jamás, never. Even Magda wasn't too hot on the rapprochement at first, but I had the momentum of the past on my side. When she asked me, Why don't you leave me alone? I told her the truth: It's because I love you, mami. I know this sounds like a load of doo-doo, but it's true: Magda's my heart. I didn't want her to leave me; I wasn't about to start looking for a girlfriend because I'd fucked up one lousy time.

Don't think it was a cakewalk, because it wasn't. Magda's stubborn; back when we first started dating, she said she wouldn't sleep with me until we'd been together at least a month, and homegirl stuck to it, no matter how hard I tried to get into her knickknacks. She's sensitive, too. Takes to hurt the way water takes to paper. You can't imagine how many times she asked (especially after we finished fucking), Were you ever going to tell me? This and Why? were her favorite questions. My favorite answers were Yes and It was a stupid mistake. I wasn't thinking.

We even had some conversation about Cassandra—usually in the dark, when we couldn't see each other. Magda asked me if I'd loved Cassandra and I told her, No, I didn't. Do you still think about her? Nope. Did you like fucking her? To be honest, baby, it was lousy. That one is never very believable but you got to say it anyway no matter how stupid and unreal it sounds: say it.

And for a while after we got back together everything was as fine as it could be.

But only for a little while. Slowly, almost imperceptibly my Magda started turning into another Magda. Who didn't want to sleep over as much or scratch my back when I asked her to.

Amazing what you notice. Like how she never used to ask me to call back when she was on the line with somebody else. I always had priority. Not anymore. So of course I blamed all that shit on her girls, who I knew for a fact were still feeding her a bad line about me.

She wasn't the only one with counsel. My boys were like, Fuck her, don't sweat that bitch, but every time I tried I couldn't pull it off. I was into Magda for real. I started working overtime on her again, but nothing seemed to pan out. Every movie we went to, every night drive we took, every time she did sleep over seemed to confirm something negative about me. I felt like I was dying by degrees, but when I brought it up she told me that I was being paranoid.

About a month later, she started making the sort of changes that would have alarmed a paranoid nigger. Cuts her hair, buys better makeup, rocks new clothes, goes out dancing on Friday nights with her friends. When I ask her if we can chill, I'm no longer sure it's a done deal. A lot of the time she Bartlebys me, says, No, I'd rather not. I ask her what the hell she thinks this is and she says, That's what I'm trying to figure out.

I know what she was doing. Making me aware of my precarious position in her life. Like I was not aware.

Then it was June. Hot white clouds stranded in the sky, cars being washed down with hoses, music allowed outside. Everybody getting ready for summer, even us. We'd planned a trip to Santo Domingo early in the year, an anniversary present, and

THE SUN, THE MOON, THE STARS

had to decide whether we were still going or not. It had been on the horizon awhile, but I figured it was something that would resolve itself. When it didn't, I brought the tickets out and asked her, How do you feel about it?

Like it's too much of a commitment.

Could be worse. It's a vacation, for Christ's sake.

I see it as pressure.

Doesn't have to be pressure.

I don't know why I get stuck on it the way I do. Bringing it up every day, trying to get her to commit. Maybe I was getting tired of the situation we were in. Wanted to flex, wanted something to change. Or maybe I'd gotten this idea in my head that if she said, Yes, we're going, then shit would be fine between us. If she said, No, it's not for me, then at least I'd know that it was over.

Her girls, the sorest losers on the planet, advised her to take the trip and then never speak to me again. She, of course, told me this shit, because she couldn't stop herself from telling me everything she's thinking. How do you feel about that suggestion? I asked her.

She shrugged. It's an idea.

Even my boys were like, Nigger, sounds like you're wasting a whole lot of loot on some bullshit, but I really thought it would be good for us. Deep down, where my boys don't know me, I'm an optimist. I thought, Me and her on the Island. What couldn't this cure?

LET ME CONFESS: I love Santo Domingo. I love coming home to the guys in blazers trying to push little cups of Brugal into my hands. Love the plane landing, everybody clapping when the wheels kiss the runway. Love the fact that I'm the only nigger on board without a Cuban link or a flapjack of makeup on my face. Love the redhead woman on her way to meet the daughter she hasn't seen in eleven years. The gifts she holds on her lap, like the bones of a saint. M'ija has tetas now, the woman whispers to her neighbor. Last time I saw her, she could barely speak in sentences. Now she's a woman. Imagínate. I love the bags my mother packs, shit for relatives and something for Magda, a gift. You give this to her no matter what happens.

If this was another kind of story, I'd tell you about the sea. What it looks like after it's been forced into the sky through a blowhole. How when I'm driving in from the airport and see it like this, like shredded silver, I know I'm back for real. I'd tell you how many poor motherfuckers there are. More albinos, more cross-eyed niggers, more tígueres than you'll ever see. And I'd tell you about the traffic: the entire history of late-twentieth-century automobiles swarming across every flat stretch of ground, a cosmology of battered cars, battered motorcycles, battered trucks, and battered buses, and an equal number of repair shops, run by any fool with a wrench. I'd tell you

THE SUN, THE MOON, THE STARS

9

about the shanties and our no-running-water faucets and the sambos on the billboards and the fact that my family house comes equipped with an ever-reliable latrine. I'd tell you about my abuelo and his campo hands, how unhappy he is that I'm not sticking around, and I'd tell you about the street where I was born, Calle XXI, how it hasn't decided yet if it wants to be a slum or not and how it's been in this state of indecision for years.

But that would make it another kind of story, and I'm having enough trouble with this one as it is. You'll have to take my word for it. Santo Domingo is Santo Domingo. Let's pretend we all know what goes on there.

I MUST HAVE been smoking dust, because I thought we were fine those first couple of days. Sure, staying locked up at my abuelo's house bored Magda to tears, she even said so—I'm bored, Yunior—but I'd warned her about the obligatory Visit with Abuelo. I thought she wouldn't mind; she's normally mad cool with the viejitos. But she didn't say much to him. Just fidgeted in the heat and drank fifteen bottles of water. Point is, we were out of the capital and on a guagua to the interior before the second day had even begun. The landscapes were superfly—even though there was a drought on and the whole campo, even the houses, was covered in that red dust. There I was. Pointing out all the shit that had changed since the year before. The new Pizzarelli and the little plastic bags of water the tigueritos were selling. Even kicked the historicals. This is where Trujillo and his Marine pals slaughtered the gavilleros, here's where the Jefe used to take his girls, here's where Balaguer sold his soul to the Devil. And Magda seemed to be enjoying herself. Nodded her head. Talked back a little. What can I tell you? I thought we were on a positive vibe.

I guess when I look back there were signs. First off, Magda's not quiet. She's a talker, a fucking boca, and we used to have this thing where I would lift my hand and say, Time out, and she would have to be quiet for at least two minutes, just so I could process some of the information she'd been spouting. She'd be embarrassed and chastened, but not so embarrassed and chastened that when I said, OK, time's up, she didn't launch right into it again.

Maybe it was my good mood. It was like the first time in weeks that I felt relaxed, that I wasn't acting like something was about to give at any moment. It bothered me that she insisted on reporting to her girls every night—like they were expecting me to kill her or something—but, fuck it, I still thought we were doing better than anytime before.

We were in this crazy budget hotel near Pucamaima. I was standing on the balcony staring at the Septentrionales and the blacked-out city when I heard her crying. I thought it was something serious, found the flashlight, and fanned the light over her heat-swollen face. Are you OK?

She shook her head. I don't want to be here.

What do you mean?

What don't you understand? I. Don't. Want. To. Be. Here.

This was not the Magda I knew. The Magda I knew was super courteous. Knocked on a door before she opened it.

I almost shouted, What is your fucking problem! But I didn't. I ended up hugging and babying her and asking her what was wrong. She cried for a long time and then after a silence started talking. By then the lights had flickered back on. Turned out she didn't want to travel around like a hobo. I thought we'd be on a beach, she said.

We're going to be on a beach. The day after tomorrow.

Can't we go now?

What could I do? She was in her underwear, waiting for me to say something. So what jumped out of my mouth? Baby, we'll do whatever you want. I called the hotel in La Romana, asked if we could come early, and the next morning I put us on an express guagua to the capital and then a second one to La Romana. I didn't say a fucking word to her and she didn't say nothing to me. She seemed tired and watched the world outside like maybe she was expecting it to speak to her.

By the middle of Day 3 of our All-Quisqueya Redemption Tour we were in an air-conditioned bungalow watching HBO.

Exactly where I want to be when I'm in Santo Domingo. In a fucking resort. Magda was reading a book by a Trappist, in a better mood, I guessed, and I was sitting on the edge of the bed, fingering my useless map.

I was thinking, For this I deserve something nice. Something physical. Me and Magda were pretty damn casual about sex, but since the breakup shit has gotten weird. First of all, it ain't regular like before. I'm lucky to score some once a week. I have to nudge her, start things up, or we won't fuck at all. And she plays like she doesn't want it, and sometimes she doesn't and then I have to cool it, but other times she does want it and I have to touch her pussy, which is my way of initiating things, of saying, So, how about we kick it, mami? And she'll turn her head, which is her way of saying, I'm too proud to acquiesce openly to your animal desires, but if you continue to put your finger in me I won't stop you.

Today we started no problem, but then halfway through she said, Wait, we shouldn't.

I wanted to know why.

She closed her eyes like she was embarrassed at herself. Forget about it, she said, moving her hips under me. Just forget about it.

I DON'T EVEN want to tell you where we're at. We're in Casa de Campo. The Resort That Shame Forgot. The average asshole would love this place. It's the largest, wealthiest resort on the Island, which means it's a goddamn fortress, walled away from everybody else. Guachimanes and peacocks and ambitious topiaries everywhere. Advertises itself in the States as its own country, and it might as well be. Has its own airport, thirty-six holes of golf, beaches so white they ache to be trampled, and the only Island Dominicans you're guaranteed to see are either caked up or changing your sheets. Let's just say my abuelo has never been here, and neither has yours. This is where the Garcías and the Colóns come to relax after a long month of oppressing the masses, where the tutumpotes can trade tips with their colleagues from abroad. Chill here too long and you'll be sure to have your ghetto pass revoked, no questions asked.

We wake up bright and early for the buffet, get served by cheerful women in Aunt Jemima costumes. I shit you not: these sisters even have to wear hankies on their heads. Magda is scratching out a couple of cards to her family. I want to talk about the day before, but when I bring it up she puts down her pen. Jams on her shades.

I feel like you're pressuring me.

How am I pressuring you? I ask.

I just want some space to myself every now and then. Every time I'm with you I have this sense that you want something from me.

Time to yourself, I say. What does that mean?

Like maybe once a day, you do one thing, I do another.

Like when? Now?

It doesn't have to be now. She looks exasperated. Why don't we just go down to the beach?

As we walk over to the courtesy golf cart, I say, I feel like you rejected my whole country, Magda.

Don't be ridiculous. She drops one hand in my lap. I just wanted to relax. What's wrong with that?

The sun is blazing and the blue of the ocean is an overload on the brain. Casa de Campo has got beaches the way the rest of the Island has got problems. These, though, have no merengue, no little kids, nobody trying to sell you chicharrones, and there's a massive melanin deficit in evidence. Every fifty feet there's at least one Eurofuck beached out on a towel like some scary pale monster that the sea's vomited up. They look like philosophy professors, like budget Foucaults, and too many of them are in the company of a dark-assed Dominican girl. I mean it, these girls can't be no more than sixteen, look puro ingenio to me. You can tell by their inability to communicate that these two didn't meet back in their Left Bank days.

Magda's rocking a dope Ochun-colored bikini that her girls helped her pick out so she could torture me, and I'm in these old ruined trunks that say "Sandy Hook Forever!" I'll admit it, with Magda half naked in public I'm feeling vulnerable and uneasy. I put my hand on her knee. I just wish you'd say you love me.

Yunior, please.

Can you say you like me a lot?

Can you leave me alone? You're such a pestilence.

I let the sun stake me out to the sand. It's disheartening, me and Magda together. We don't look like a couple. When she smiles niggers ask her for her hand in marriage; when I smile folks check their wallets. Magda's been a star the whole time we've been here. You know how it is when you're on the Island and your girl's an octoroon. Brothers go apeshit. On buses, the machos were like, Tú sí eres bella, muchacha. Every time I dip into the water for a swim, some Mediterranean Messenger of Love starts rapping to her. Of course, I'm not polite. Why don't you beat it, pancho? We're on our honeymoon here. There's this one squid who's mad persistent, even sits down near us so he can impress her with the hair around his nipples, and instead of ignoring him she starts a conversation and it turns out he's Dominican, too, from Quisqueya Heights, an assistant DA who loves his people. Better I'm their prosecutor, he says. At least I understand them. I'm thinking he sounds like the sort of nigger who in the old days used to lead bwana to the rest of us. After three minutes of him, I can't take it no more, and say, Magda, stop talking to that asshole.

The assistant DA startles. I know you ain't talking to me, he says.

Actually, I say, I am.

This is unbelievable. Magda gets to her feet and walks

stiff-legged toward the water. She's got a half-moon of sand stuck to her butt. A total fucking heartbreak.

Homeboy's saying something else to me, but I'm not listening. I already know what she'll say when she sits back down. Time for you to do your thing and me to do mine.

THAT NIGHT I LOITER around the pool and the local bar, Club Cacique, Magda nowhere to be found. I meet a dominicana from West New York. Fly, of course. Trigueña, with the most outrageous perm this side of Dyckman. Lucy is her name. She's hanging out with three of her teenage girl cousins. When she removes her robe to dive into the pool, I see a spiderweb of scars across her stomach.

I also meet these two rich older dudes drinking cognac at the bar. Introduce themselves as the Vice-President and Bárbaro, his bodyguard. I must have the footprint of fresh disaster on my face. They listen to my troubles like they're a couple of capos and I'm talking murder. They commiserate. It's a thousand degrees out and the mosquitoes hum like they're about to inherit the earth, but both these cats are wearing expensive suits, and Bárbaro is even sporting a purple ascot. Once a soldier tried to saw open his neck and now he covers the scar. I'm a modest man, he says.

I go off to phone the room. No Magda. I check with reception. No messages. I return to the bar and smile.

The Vice-President is a young brother, in his late thirties, and pretty cool for a chupabarrio. He advises me to find another woman. Make her bella and negra. I think, Cassandra.

The Vice-President waves his hand and shots of Barceló appear so fast you'd think it's science fiction.

Jealousy is the best way to jump-start a relationship, the Vice-President says. I learned that when I was a student at Syracuse. Dance with another woman, dance merengue with her, and see if your jeva's not roused to action.

You mean roused to violence.

She hit you?

When I first told her. She smacked me right across the chops.

Pero, hermano, why'd you tell her? Bárbaro wants to know. Why didn't you just deny it?

Compadre, she received a letter. It had evidence.

The Vice-President smiles fantastically and I can see why he's a vice-president. Later, when I get home, I'll tell my mother about this whole mess, and she'll tell me what this brother was the vice-president of.

They only hit you, he says, when they care.

Amen, Bárbaro murmurs. Amen.

ALL OF MAGDA'S FRIENDS SAY I cheated because I was Dominican, that all us Dominican men are dogs and can't be trusted. I doubt that I can speak for all Dominican men but I doubt they can either. From my perspective it wasn't genetics; there were reasons. Causalities.

The truth is there ain't no relationship in the world that doesn't hit turbulence. Mine and Magda's certainly did.

I was living in Brooklyn and she was with her folks in Jersey. We talked every day on the phone and on weekends we saw each other. Usually I went in. We were real Jersey, too: malls, the parents, movies, a lot of TV. After a year of us together, this was where we were at. Our relationship wasn't the sun, the moon, and the stars, but it wasn't bullshit, either. Especially not on Saturday mornings, over at my apartment, when she made us coffee campo-style, straining it through the sock thing. Told her parents the night before she was staying over at Claribel's; they must have known where she was, but they never said shit. I'd sleep late and she'd read, scratching my back in slow arcs, and when I was ready to get up I would start kissing her until she would say, God, Yunior, you're making me wet.

I wasn't unhappy and wasn't actively pursuing ass like some niggers. Sure, I checked out other females, even danced with them when I went out, but I wasn't keeping numbers or nothing.

Still, it's not like seeing somebody once a week doesn't cool shit out, because it does. Nothing you'd really notice until some new chick arrives at your job with a big butt and a smart mouth and she's like on you almost immediately, touching your pectorals, moaning about some moreno she's dating who's always treating her like shit, saying, Black guys don't understand Spanish girls.

Cassandra. She organized the football pool and did crossword puzzles while she talked on the phone, and had a thing for denim skirts. We got into a habit of going to lunch and having the same conversation. I advised her to drop the moreno, she advised me to find a girlfriend who could fuck. First week of knowing her, I made the mistake of telling her that sex with Magda had never been top-notch.

God, I feel sorry for you, Cassandra said. At least Rupert gives me some Grade A dick.

The first night we did it—and it was good, too, she wasn't false advertising—I felt so lousy that I couldn't sleep, even though she was one of those sisters whose body fits next to you perfect. I was like, She knows, so I called Magda right from the bed and asked her if she was OK.

You sound strange, she said.

I remember Cassandra pressing the hot cleft of her pussy against my leg and me saying, I just miss you.

ANOTHER PERFECT SUNNY CARIBBEAN DAY, and the only thing Magda has said is Give me the lotion. Tonight the resort is throwing a party. All guests are invited. Attire's semiformal, but I don't have the clothes or the energy to dress up. Magda, though, has both. She pulls on these super-tight gold lamé pants and a matching halter that shows off her belly ring. Her hair is shiny and as dark as night and I can remember the first time I kissed those curls, asking her, Where are the stars? And she said, They're a little lower, papi.

We both end up in front of the mirror. I'm in slacks and a wrinkled chacabana. She's applying her lipstick; I've always believed that the universe invented the color red solely for Latinas.

We look good, she says.

It's true. My optimism is starting to come back. I'm thinking, This is the night for reconciliation. I put my arms around her, but she drops her bomb without blinking a fucking eye: tonight, she says, she needs space.

My arms drop.

I knew you'd be pissed, she says.

You're a real bitch, you know that.

I didn't want to come here. You made me.

If you didn't want to come, why didn't you have the fucking guts to say so?

And on and on and on, until finally I just say, Fuck this, and head out. I feel unmoored and don't have a clue of what comes next. This is the endgame, and instead of pulling out all the stops, instead of pongándome más chivo que un

THE SUN, THE MOON, THE STARS

chivo, I'm feeling sorry for myself, como un parigüayo sin suerte. I'm thinking over and over, I'm not a bad guy, I'm not a bad guy.

Club Cacique is jammed. I'm looking for that girl Lucy. I find the Vice-President and Bárbaro instead. At the quiet end of the bar, they're drinking cognac and arguing about whether there are fifty-six Dominicans in the major leagues or fifty-seven. They clear out a space for me and clap me on the shoulder.

This place is killing me, I say.

How dramatic. The Vice-President reaches into his suit for his keys. He's wearing those Italian leather shoes that look like braided slippers. Are you inclined to ride with us?

Sure, I say. Why the fuck not?

I wish to show you the birthplace of our nation.

Before we leave I check out the crowd. Lucy has arrived. She's alone at the edge of the bar in a fly black dress. Smiles excitedly, lifts her arm, and I can see the dark stubbled spot in her armpit. She's got sweat patches over her outfit and mosquito bites on her beautiful arms. I think, I should stay, but my legs carry me right out of the club.

We pile in a diplomat's black BMW. I'm in the backseat with Bárbaro; the Vice-President's up front driving. We leave Casa de Campo behind and the frenzy of La Romana, and soon everything starts smelling of processed cane. The roads are dark—I'm talking no fucking lights—and in our beams the bugs swarm like a biblical plague. We're passing the cognac around. I'm with a vice-president, I figure what the fuck.

He's talking—about his time in upstate New York—but so is Bárbaro. The bodyguard's suit's rumpled and his hand shakes as he smokes his cigarettes. Some fucking bodyguard. He's telling me about his childhood in San Juan, near the border of Haiti. Liborio's country. I wanted to be an engineer, he tells me. I wanted to build schools and hospitals for the pueblo. I'm not really listening to him; I'm thinking about Magda, how I'll probably never taste her chocha again.

And then we're out of the car, stumbling up a slope, through bushes and guineo and bamboo, and the mosquitoes are chewing us up like we're the special of the day. Bárbaro's got a huge flashlight, a darkness obliterator. The Vice-President's cursing, trampling through the underbrush, saying, It's around here somewhere. This is what I get for being in office so long. It's only then I notice that Bárbaro's holding a huge fucking machine gun and his hand ain't shaking no more. He isn't watching me or the Vice-President—he's listening. I'm not scared, but this is getting a little too freaky for me.

What kind of gun is that? I ask, by way of conversation.

A P-90.

What the fuck is that?

Something old made new.

Great, I'm thinking, a philosopher.

It's here, the Vice-President calls out.

I creep over and see that he's standing over a hole in the ground. The earth is red. Bauxite. And the hole is blacker than any of us.

This is the Cave of the Jagua, the Vice-President announces in a deep, respectful voice. The birthplace of the Taínos.

I raise my eyebrow. I thought they were South American.

We're speaking mythically here.

Bárbaro points the light down the hole but that doesn't improve anything.

Would you like to see inside? the Vice-President asks me.

I must have said yes, because Bárbaro gives me the flashlight and the two of them grab me by my ankles and lower me into the hole. All my coins fly out of my pockets. Bendiciones. I don't see much, just some odd colors on the eroded walls, and the Vice-President's calling down, Isn't it beautiful?

This is the perfect place for insight, for a person to become somebody better. The Vice-President probably saw his future self hanging in this darkness, bulldozing the poor out of their shanties, and Bárbaro, too—buying a concrete house for his mother, showing her how to work the air-conditioner—but, me, all I can manage is a memory of the first time me and Magda talked. Back at Rutgers. We were waiting for an E bus together on George Street and she was wearing purple. All sorts of purple.

And that's when I know it's over. As soon as you start thinking about the beginning, it's the end.

THIS IS HOW YOU LOSE HER

I cry, and when they pull me up the Vice-President says, indignantly, God, you don't have to be a pussy about it.

THAT MUST HAVE been some serious Island voodoo: the ending I saw in the cave came true. The next day we went back to the United States. Five months later I got a letter from my ex-baby. I was dating someone new, but Magda's handwriting still blasted every molecule of air out of my lungs.

It turned out she was also going out with somebody else. A very nice guy she'd met. Dominican, like me. *Except he loves me*, she wrote.

But I'm getting ahead of myself. I need to finish by showing you what kind of fool I was.

When I returned to the bungalow that night, Magda was waiting up for me. Was packed, looked like she'd been bawling.

I'm going home tomorrow, she said.

I sat down next to her. Took her hand. This can work, I said. All we have to do is try.

Nilda

NILDA WAS MY BROTHER'S GIRLFRIEND.
This is how all these stories begin.

She was Dominican, from here, and had super-long hair, like those Pentecostal girls, and a chest you wouldn't believe— I'm talking world-class. Rafa would sneak her down into our basement bedroom after our mother went to bed and do her to whatever was on the radio right then. The two of them had to let me stay, because if my mother heard me upstairs on the couch everybody's ass would have been fried. And since I wasn't about to spend my night out in the bushes this is how it was.

Rafa didn't make no noise, just a low something that resembled breathing. Nilda was the one. She seemed to be trying to hold back from crying the whole time. It was crazy hearing her like that. The Nilda I'd grown up with was one of the quietest girls you'd ever meet. She let her hair wall away her face and read *The New Mutants,* and the only time she looked straight at anything was when she looked out a window.

But that was before she'd gotten that chest, before that slash of black hair had gone from something to pull on the bus to something to stroke in the dark. The new Nilda wore stretch pants and Iron Maiden shirts; she had already run away from her mother's and ended up at a group home; she'd already slept with Toño and Nestor and Little Anthony from Parkwood, older guys. She crashed over at our apartment a lot because she hated her moms, who was the neighborhood borracha. In the morning she slipped out before my mother woke up and found her. Waited for heads at the bus stop, fronted like she'd come from her own place, same clothes as the day before and greasy hair so everybody thought her a skank. Waited for my brother and didn't talk to anybody and nobody talked to her, because she'd always been one of those quiet, semi-retarded girls who you couldn't talk to without being dragged into a whirlpool of dumb stories. If Rafa decided that he wasn't going to school then she'd wait near our apartment until my mother left for work. Sometimes Rafa let her in right away. Sometimes he slept late and she'd wait across the street, building letters out of pebbles until she saw him crossing the living room.

She had big stupid lips and a sad moonface and the driest skin. Always rubbing lotion on it and cursing the moreno father who'd given it to her.

It seemed like she was forever waiting for my brother. Nights she'd knock and I'd let her in and we'd sit on the couch while Rafa was off at his job at the carpet factory or working out at the gym. I'd show her my newest comics and she'd read them real close, but as soon as Rafa showed up she'd throw them in my lap and jump into his arms. I missed you, she'd say in a little-girl voice, and Rafa would laugh. You should have seen him in those days: he had the face bones of a saint. Then

Mami's door would open and Rafa would detach himself and cowboy-saunter over to Mami and say, You got something for me to eat, vieja? Claro que sí, Mami'd say, trying to put her glasses on.

He had us all, the way only a pretty nigger can.

Once when Rafa was late from the job and we were alone in the apartment a long time, I asked Nilda about the group home. It was three weeks before the end of the school year and everybody had entered the do-nothing stage. I was fourteen and reading *Dhalgren* for the second time; I had an IQ that would have broken you in two but I would have traded it in for a halfway decent face in a second.

It was pretty cool up there, she said. She was pulling on the front of her halter top, trying to air her chest out. The food was bad but there were a lot of cute guys in the house with me. They all wanted me.

She started chewing on a nail. Even the guys who worked there were calling me after I left, she said.

THE ONLY REASON Rafa went after her was because his last full-time girlfriend had gone back to Guyana—she was this dougla girl with a single eyebrow and skin to die for—and because Nilda had pushed up to him. She'd only been back from the group home a couple of months, but by then she'd already gotten a rep as a cuero. A lot of the Dominican girls in town were on some serious lockdown—we saw them on the bus and at school and maybe at the Pathmark, but since most families knew exactly what kind of tígueres were roaming the neighborhood these girls weren't allowed to hang out. Nilda was different. She was what we called in those days brown trash. Her moms was a mean-ass drunk and always running around South Amboy with her white boyfriends—which is a way of saying Nilda could hang and, man, did she ever. Always out in the world, always cars rolling up beside her. Before I even knew she was back from the group home she got scooped up by this older nigger from the back apartments. He kept her on his dick for almost four months, and I used to see them driving around in his fucked-up rust-eaten Sunbird while I delivered my papers. Motherfucker was like three hundred years old, but because he had a car and a record collection and foto albums from his Vietnam days and because he bought her clothes to replace the old shit she was wearing, Nilda was all lost on him.

I hated this nigger with a passion, but when it came to guys there was no talking to Nilda. I used to ask her, What's up with Wrinkle Dick? And she would get so mad she wouldn't speak to me for days, and then I'd get this note, I want you to respect my man. Whatever, I'd write back. Then the old dude bounced, no one knew where, the usual scenario in my neighborhood, and for a couple of months she got tossed by those cats from Parkwood. On Thursdays, which was comic-book day, she'd drop in to see what I'd picked up and she'd talk to me about how unhappy she was. We'd sit together until it got dark and then her beeper would fire up and she'd peer into its display and say, I have to go. Sometimes I could grab her and pull her back on the couch, and we'd stay there a long time, me waiting for her to fall in love with me, her waiting for whatever, but other times she'd be serious. I have to go see my man, she'd say.

One of those comic-book days what she saw was my brother coming back from his five-mile run. Rafa was still boxing then and he was cut up like crazy, the muscles on his chest and abdomen so striated they looked like something out of a Frazetta drawing. He noticed her because she was wearing these ridiculous shorts and this tank that couldn't have blocked a sneeze and a thin roll of stomach was poking from between the fabrics and he smiled at her and she got real serious and uncomfortable and he told her to fix him some iced tea and she told him to fix it himself. You a guest here, he said. You should be earning your fucking keep. He went into the shower and as soon as he did she was in the kitchen stirring and I told her to leave it, but she said, I might as well. We drank all of it.

I wanted to warn her, tell her he was a monster, but she was already headed for him at the speed of light.

The next day Rafa's car turned up broken—what a coincidence—so he took the bus to school and when he was walking past our seat he took her hand and pulled her to her feet and she said, Get off me. Her eyes were pointed straight at the floor. I just want to show you something, he said. She was pulling with her arm but the rest of her was ready to go. Come on, Rafa said, and finally she went. Save my seat, she said over her shoulder, and I was like, Don't worry about it. Before we even swung onto 516 Nilda was in my brother's lap and he had his hand so far up her skirt it looked like he was performing a surgical procedure. When we were getting off the bus Rafa pulled me aside and held his hand in front of my nose. Smell this, he said. This is what's wrong with women.

You couldn't get anywhere near Nilda for the rest of the day. She had her hair pulled back and was glorious with triumph. Even the whitegirls knew about my overmuscled about-to-be-a-senior brother and were impressed. And while Nilda sat at the end of our lunch table and whispered to some girls, me and my boys ate our crap sandwiches and talked about the X-Men—this was back when the X-Men still made some kind of sense—and even if we didn't want to admit it the truth was now patent and awful: all the real dope girls were headed up to the high school, like moths to a light, and there was nothing any of us younger cats could do about it. My man José Negrón—aka Joe Black—took Nilda's defection the hardest, since he'd actually imagined he had a chance with her. Right after she got back from the group home he'd held her hand on the bus, and even though she'd gone off with other guys, he'd never forgotten it.

I was in the basement three nights later when she and Rafa did it. That first time neither of them made a sound.

THEY WENT OUT that whole summer. I don't remember anyone doing anything big. Me and my pathetic little crew hiked over to Morgan Creek and swam around in water stinking of leachate from the landfill; we were just getting serious about the licks that year and Joe Black was stealing bottles out of his father's stash and we were drinking them down to the corners on the swings behind the apartments. Because of the heat and because of what I felt inside my chest a lot, I often just sat in the crib with my brother and Nilda. Rafa was tired all the time and pale: this had happened in a matter of days. I used to say, Look at you, whiteboy, and he used to say, Look at you, you black ugly nigger. He didn't feel like doing much, and besides his car had finally broken down for real, so we would all sit in the air-conditioned apartment and watch TV. Rafa had decided he wasn't going back to school for his senior year, and even though my moms was heartbroken and trying to guilt him into it five times a day, this was all he talked about. School had never been his gig, and after my pops left us for his twenty-five-year-old Rafa didn't feel he needed to pretend any longer. I'd like to take a long fucking trip, he told us. See California before it slides into the ocean. California, I said. California, he said. A nigger could make a showing out there. I'd like to go there, too, Nilda said, but Rafa didn't answer her. He had closed his eyes and you could see he was in pain.

We rarely talked about our father. Me, I was just happy not to be getting my ass kicked in anymore but once right at the beginning of the Last Great Absence I asked my brother where he thought he was, and Rafa said, Like I fucking care.

End of conversation. World without end.

On days niggers were really out of their minds with boredom we trooped down to the pool and got in for free because Rafa was boys with one of the lifeguards. I swam, Nilda went on missions around the pool just so she could show off how tight she looked in her bikini, and Rafa sprawled under the awning and took it all in. Sometimes he called me over and we'd sit together for a while and he'd close his eyes and I'd watch the water dry on my ashy legs and then he'd tell me to go back to the pool. When Nilda finished promenading and came back to where Rafa was chilling she kneeled at his side and he would kiss her real long, his hands playing up and down the length of her back. Ain't nothing like a fifteen-year-old with a banging body, those hands seemed to be saying, at least to me.

Joe Black was always watching them. Man, he muttered, she's so fine I'd lick her asshole *and* tell you niggers about it.

Maybe I would have thought they were cute if I hadn't known Rafa. He might have seemed enamorao with Nilda but he also had mad girls in orbit. Like this one piece of white trash from Sayreville, and this morena from Nieuw Amsterdam Village who also slept over and sounded like a freight train when they did it. I don't remember her name, but I do remember how her perm shone in the glow of our night-light.

In August Rafa quit his job at the carpet factory—I'm too fucking tired, he complained, and some mornings his leg bones hurt so much he couldn't get out of bed right away. The Romans used to shatter these with iron clubs, I told him while I massaged his shins. The pain would kill you instantly. Great, he said. Cheer me up some more, you fucking bastard. One day Mami took him to the hospital for a checkup and afterward I found them sitting on the couch, both of them dressed up, watching TV like nothing had happened. They were holding hands and Mami appeared tiny next to him.

Well?

Rafa shrugged. The doc thinks I'm anemic.

Anemic ain't bad.

Yeah, Rafa said, laughing bitterly. God bless Medicaid.

In the light of the TV, he looked terrible.

THAT WAS THE SUMMER when everything we would become was hovering just over our heads. Girls were starting to take notice of me; I wasn't good-looking but I listened and had boxing muscles in my arms. In another universe I probably came out OK, ended up with mad novias and jobs and a sea of love in which to swim, but in this world I had a brother who was dying of cancer and a long dark patch of life like a mile of black ice waiting for me up ahead.

One night, a couple of weeks before school started—they must have thought I was asleep—Nilda started telling Rafa about her plans for the future. I think even she knew what was about to happen. Listening to her imagining herself was about the saddest thing you ever heard. How she wanted to get away from her moms and open up a group home for runaway kids. But this one would be real cool, she said. It would be for normal kids who just got problems. She must have loved him because she went on and on. Plenty of people talk about having a flow, but that night I really heard one, something that was unbroken, that fought itself and worked together all at once. Rafa didn't say nothing. Maybe he had his hands in her hair or maybe he was just like, Fuck you. When she finished he didn't even say wow. I wanted to kill myself with embarrassment. About a half hour later she got up and dressed. She couldn't see me or she would have known that I thought she was beautiful. She stepped into her pants and pulled them up in one motion, sucked in her stomach while she buttoned them. I'll see you later, she said.

Yeah, he said.

After she walked out he put on the radio and started on the speed bag. I stopped pretending I was asleep; I sat up and watched him.

Did you guys have a fight or something?

No, he said.

Why'd she leave?

He sat down on my bed. His chest was sweating. She had to go.

But where's she gonna stay?

I don't know. He put his hand on my face, gently. Why ain't you minding your business?

A week later he was seeing some other girl. She was from Trinidad, a cocoa pañyol, and she had this phony-as-hell English accent. It was the way we all were back then. None of us wanted to be niggers. Not for nothing.

I GUESS TWO YEARS PASSED. My brother was gone by then, and I was on my way to becoming a nut. I was out of school most of the time and had no friends and I sat inside and watched Univision or walked down to the dump and smoked the mota I should have been selling until I couldn't see. Nilda didn't fare so well, either. A lot of the things that happened to her, though, had nothing to do with me or my brother. She fell in love a couple more times, really bad with this one moreno truck driver who took her to Manalapan and then abandoned her at the end of the summer. I had to drive over to get her, and the house was one of those tiny box jobs with a fifty-cent lawn and no kind of charm; she was acting like she was some

Italian chick and offered me a paso in the car, but I put my hand on hers and told her to stop it. Back home she fell in with more stupid niggers, relocated kids from the City, and they came at her with drama and some of their girls beat her up, a Brick City beat-down, and she lost her bottom front teeth. She was in and out of school and for a while they put her on home instruction, and that was when she finally dropped.

My junior year she started delivering papers so she could make money, and since I was spending a lot of time outside I saw her every now and then. Broke my heart. She wasn't at her lowest yet but she was aiming there and when we passed each other she always smiled and said hi. She was starting to put on weight and she'd cut her hair down to nothing and her moon-face was heavy and alone. I always said Wassup and when I had cigarettes I gave them to her. She'd gone to the funeral, along with a couple of his other girls, and what a skirt she'd worn, like maybe she could still convince him of something, and she'd kissed my mother but the vieja hadn't known who she was. I had to tell Mami on the ride home and all she could remember about her was that she was the one who smelled good. It wasn't until Mami said it that I realized it was true.

IT WAS ONLY ONE SUMMER and she was nobody special, so what's the point of all this? He's gone, he's gone, he's gone. I'm twenty-three and I'm washing my clothes up at the mini mall on Ernston Road. She's here with me—she's folding her shit and smiling and showing me her missing teeth and saying, It's been a long time, hasn't it, Yunior?

Years, I say, loading my whites. Outside, the sky is clear of gulls, and down at the apartment my moms is waiting for me with dinner. Six months earlier we were sitting in front of the TV and my mother said, Well, I think I'm finally over this place.

Nilda asks, Did you move or something?

I shake my head. Just been working.

God, it's been a long, long time. She's on her clothes like magic, making everything neat, making everything fit. There are four other people at the counters, broke-ass-looking niggers with kneesocks and croupier's hats and scars snaking up their arms, and they all seem like sleepwalkers compared with her. She shakes her head, grinning. Your brother, she says.

Rafa.

She points her finger at me like my brother always did.

I miss him sometimes.

She nods. Me, too. He was a good guy to me.

I must have disbelief on my face because she finishes shaking out her towels and then stares straight through me. He treated me the best.

Nilda.

He used to sleep with my hair over his face. He used to say it made him feel safe.

What else can we say? She finishes her stacking, I hold the door open for her. The locals watch us leave. We walk back through the old neighborhood, slowed down by the bulk of our clothes. London Terrace has changed now that the landfill has shut down. Kicked-up rents and mad South Asian people and whitefolks living in the apartments, but it's our kids you see in the streets and hanging from the porches.

Nilda is watching the ground as though she's afraid she might fall. My heart is beating and I think, We could do anything. We could marry. We could drive off to the West Coast. We could start over. It's all possible but neither of us speaks for a long time and the moment closes and we're back in the world we've always known.

Remember the day we met? she asks.

I nod.

You wanted to play baseball.

It was summer, I say. You were wearing a tank top.

You made me put on a shirt before you'd let me be on your team. Do you remember?

I remember, I say.

We never spoke again. A couple of years later I went away to college and I don't know where the fuck she went.

Alma

YOU, YUNIOR, HAVE A GIRLFRIEND named Alma, who has a long tender horse neck and a big Dominican ass that seems to exist in a fourth dimension beyond jeans. An ass that could drag the moon out of orbit. An ass she never liked until she met you. Ain't a day that passes that you don't want to press your face against that ass or bite the delicate sliding tendons of her neck. You love how she shivers when you bite, how she fights you with those arms that are so skinny they belong on an after-school special.

Alma is a Mason Gross student, one of those Sonic Youth, comic-book-reading alternatinas without whom you might never have lost your virginity. Grew up in Hoboken, part of the Latino community that got its heart burned out in the eighties, tenements turning to flame. Spent nearly every teenage day on the Lower East Side, thought it would always be home, but then NYU and Columbia both said nyet, and she ended up even farther from the city than before. Alma is in a painting phase, and the people she paints are all the color of mold, look like they've just been dredged from the bottom of a lake. Her last painting was of you, slouching against the front door: only your frowning I-had-a-lousy-Third-World-childhood-and-all-I-got-was-this-attitude eyes recognizable. She did give you one huge forearm. *I told you I'd get the muscles in.* The past couple of weeks, now that the warm is here, Alma has abandoned black, started wearing these nothing dresses made out of what feels like tissue paper; it wouldn't take more than a strong wind to undress her. She says she does it for you: *I'm reclaiming my Dominican heritage* (which ain't a complete lie—she's even taking Spanish to better minister to your moms), and when you see her on the street, flaunting, flaunting, you know exactly what every nigger that walks by is thinking because you are thinking it, too.

Alma is slender as a reed, you a steroid-addicted block; Alma loves driving, you books; Alma owns a Saturn, you have no points on your license; Alma's nails are too dirty for cooking, your spaghetti con pollo is the best in the land. You are so very different—she rolls her eyes every time you turn on the news and says she can't "stand" politics. She won't even call herself Hispanic. She brags to her girls that you're a "radical" and a real Dominican (even though on the Plátano Index you wouldn't rank, Alma being only the third Latina you've ever really dated). You brag to your boys that she has more albums than any of them do, that she says terrible whitegirl things while you fuck. She's more adventurous in bed than any girl you've had; on your first date she asked you if you wanted to come on her tits or her face, and maybe during boy training you didn't get one of the memos but you were, like, umm, neither. And at least once a week she will kneel on the mattress before you and, with one hand pulling at her dark nipples, will play with herself, not letting you touch at all, fingers whisking the soft of her and her face looking desperately, furiously happy. She loves to talk while she's being dirty, too, will whisper, You like watching me don't you, you like listening to me come, and when she finishes lets out this long demolished groan and only then will she allow you to pull her into an embrace as she wipes her gummy fingers on your chest.

Yes—it's an opposites-attract sort of thing, it's a great-sex sort of thing, it's a no-thinking sort of thing. It's wonderful! Wonderful! Until one June day Alma discovers that you are also fucking this beautiful freshman girl named Laxmi, discovers the fucking of Laxmi because she, Alma, the girlfriend, opens your journal and reads. (Oh, she had her suspicions.) She waits for you on the stoop, and when you pull up in her Saturn and notice the journal in her hand your heart plunges through you like a fat bandit through a hangman's trap. You take your time turning off the car. You are overwhelmed by a pelagic sadness. Sadness at being caught, at the incontrovertible knowledge that she will never forgive you. You stare at her incredible legs and between them, to that even more incredible pópola you've loved so inconstantly these past eight months. Only when she starts walking over in anger do you finally step out. You dance across the lawn, powered by the last fumes of your outrageous sinvergüencería. Hey, muñeca, you say, pre-varicating to the end. When she starts shrieking, you ask her, Darling, what ever is the matter? She calls you:

> a cocksucker
> a punk motherfucker
> a fake-ass Dominican.

She claims:
> you have a little penis
> no penis
> and worst of all that you like curried pussy.

(which really is unfair, you try to say, since Laxmi is from Guyana, but Alma isn't listening.)

Instead of lowering your head and copping to it like a man, you pick up the journal as one might hold a baby's beshatted diaper, as one might pinch a recently benutted condom. You glance at the offending passages. Then you look at her and smile a smile your dissembling face will remember until the day you die. Baby, you say, baby, this is part of my novel.

This is how you lose her.

Otravida,
Otravez

H E SITS ON THE MATTRESS, the fat spread of his ass popping my fitted sheets from their corners. His clothes are stiff from the cold, and the splatter of dried paint on his pants has frozen into rivets. He smells of bread. He's been talking about the house he wants to buy, how hard it is to find one when you're Latino. When I ask him to stand up so I can fix the bed, he walks over to the window. So much snow, he says. I nod and wish he would be quiet. Ana Iris is trying to sleep on the other side of the room. She has spent half the night praying for her children back in Samaná, and I know that in the morning she has to work at the fábrica. She moves uneasily, buried beneath comforters, her head beneath a pillow. Even here in the States she drapes mosquito netting over her bed.

There's a truck trying to turn the corner, he tells me. I wouldn't want to be that chamaco.

It's a busy street, I say, and it is. Mornings I find the salt and cut rock that the trucks spill onto the front lawn, little piles of treasure in the snow. Lie down, I tell him, and he comes to me, slipping under the covers. His clothes are rough and I wait until it is warm enough under the sheets before I release the buckle to his pants. We shiver together and he does not touch me until we stop.

Yasmin, he says. His mustache is against my ear, sawing at me. We had a man die today at the bread factory. He doesn't speak for a moment, as if the silence is the elastic that will bring his next words forward. Este tipo fell from the rafters. Héctor found him between the conveyors.

Was he a friend?

This one. I recruited him at a bar. Told him he wouldn't get cheated.

That's too bad, I say. I hope he doesn't have a family.

Probably does.

Did you see him?

What do you mean?

Did you see him dead?

No. I called the manager and he told me not to let anyone near. He crosses his arms. I do that roof work all the time.

You're a lucky man, Ramón.

Yes, but what if it had been me?

That's a stupid question.

What would you have done?

I set my face against him; he has known the wrong women if he expects more. I want to say, Exactly what your wife's doing in Santo Domingo. Ana Iris mutters in the corner loudly, but she's just pretending. Bailing me out of trouble. He goes quiet because he doesn't want to wake her. After a while he gets up and sits by the window. The snow has started falling again. Radio WADO says this winter will be worse than the last four, maybe the worst in ten years. I watch him: he's smoking, his fingers tracing the thin bones around his eyes, the slack of skin around his mouth. I wonder who he's thinking about. His wife, Virta, or maybe his child. He has a house in Villa Juana; I've seen the fotos Virta sent. She looks thin and sad, the dead son at her side. He keeps the pictures in a jar under his bed, very tightly sealed.

We fall asleep without kissing. Later I wake up and so does he. I ask him if he's going back to his place and he says no. The next time I wake up he doesn't. In the cold and darkness of this room he could almost be anybody. I lift his meaty hand. It is heavy and has flour under each nail. Sometimes at night I kiss his knuckles, crinkled as prunes. His hands have tasted of crackers and bread the whole three years we've been together.

HE DOES NOT TALK to me or Ana Iris as he dresses. In his top jacket pocket he carries a blue disposable razor that has begun to show rust on its sharp lip. He soaps his cheeks and chin, the water cold from the pipes, and then scrapes his face clean, trading stubble for scabs. I watch, my naked chest covered with goose bumps. He stomps downstairs and out of the house, a bit of toothpaste on his teeth. As soon as he leaves, I can hear my housemates complaining about him. Doesn't he have his own place to sleep, they'll ask me when I go into the kitchen. And I'll say yes, and smile. From the frosted window I watch him pull up his hood and hitch the triple layer of shirt, sweater, and coat onto his shoulders.

Ana Iris kicks back her covers. What are you doing? she asks me.

Nothing, I say. She watches me dress from under the craziness of her hair.

You have to learn to trust your men, she says.

I trust.

She kisses my nose, heads downstairs. I comb out my hair, sweep the crumbs and pubic hairs from my covers. Ana Iris doesn't think he'll leave me; she thinks he's too settled here, that we've been together too long. He's the sort of man who'll go to the airport but won't be able to get on board, she says. Ana Iris left her own children back on the Island, hasn't seen her three boys in nearly seven years. She understands what has to be sacrificed on a voyage.

In the bathroom I stare into my own eyes. His stubble quivers in beads of water, compass needles.

I work two blocks away, at St. Peter's Hospital. Never late. Never leave the laundry room. Never leave the heat. I load washers, I load dryers, peel the lint skin from the traps, measure out heaping scoops of crystal detergent. I'm in charge of four other workers, I make an American wage, but it's a donkey job. I sort through piles of sheets with gloved hands. The dirties are brought down by orderlies, morenas mostly. I never see the sick; they visit me through the stains and marks they leave on the sheets, the alphabet of the sick and dying. A lot of the time the stains are too deep and I have to throw these linens in the special hamper. One of the girls from Baitoa tells me she's heard that everything in the hamper gets incinerated. Because of the sida, she whispers. Sometimes the stains are rusty and old and sometimes the blood smells sharp as rain. You'd think, given the blood we see, that there's a great war going on out in the world. Just the one inside of bodies, the new girl says.

My girls are not exactly reliable, but I enjoy working with them. They play music, they feud, they tell me funny stories. And because I don't yell or bully them they like me. They're young, sent to the States by their parents. The same age I was when I arrived; they see me now, twenty-eight, five years here, as a veteran, a rock, but back then, in those first days, I was so alone that every day was like eating my own heart.

A few of the girls have boyfriends and they're the ones I'm careful about depending on. They show up late or miss weeks at a time; they move to Nueva York or Union City without warning. When that happens I have to go to the manager's office. He's a little man, a thin man, a bird-looking man; has no hair on his face, but a thatch grows on his chest and up his neck. I tell him what happened and he pulls the girl's application and rips it in half, the cleanest of sounds. In less than an hour one of the other girls has sent a friend to me for an application.

The newest girl's called Samantha and she's a problem. She's dark and heavy-browed and has a mouth like unswept glass—when you least expect it she cuts you. Walked onto the job after one of the other girls ran off to Delaware. She's been in the States only six weeks and can't believe the cold. Twice she's tipped over the detergent barrels and she has a bad habit of working without gloves and then rubbing her eyes. She tells me that she's been sick, that she's had to move twice, that her housemates have stolen her money. She has the scared, hunted look of the unlucky. Work is work, I tell her, but I loan her enough for her lunches, let her do personal laundry in our machines. I expect her to thank me, but instead she says that I talk like a man.

Does it get any better? I hear her ask the others. Just worse, they say. Wait for the freezing rain. She looks over at me, half smiling, uncertain. She's fifteen, maybe, and too thin to have mothered a child, but she's already shown me the pictures of her fat boy, Manolo. She's waiting for me to answer, me in particular because I'm the veterana, but I turn to the next load. I've tried to explain to her the trick of working hard but she doesn't seem to care. She cracks her gum and smiles at me like I'm seventy. I unfold the next sheet and like a flower the bloodstain's there, no bigger than my hand. Hamper, I say, and

Samantha throws it open. I ball the sheet up and toss. Slops right in, the loose ends dragged in by the center.

NINE HOURS OF SMOOTHING linen and I am home, eating cold yuca with hot oil, waiting for Ramón to come for me in the car he has borrowed. He is taking me to look at another house. It's been his dream since he first set foot in the States, and now, with all the jobs he's had and the money he's saved, it's possible. How many get to this point? Only the ones who never swerve, who never make mistakes, who are never unlucky. And that more or less is Ramón. He's serious about the house, which means I have to be serious about it, too. Each week we go out into the world and look. He makes an event of it, dressing like he's interviewing for a visa, drives us around the quieter sections of Paterson, where the trees have spread over roofs and garages. It's important, he says, to be careful, and I agree. He takes me with him whenever he can, but even I can tell that I'm not much help. I'm not one for change, I tell him, and I see only what's wrong with the places he wants, and later, in the car, he accuses me of sabotaging his dream, of being dura.

Tonight we're supposed to see another. He walks into the kitchen clapping his chapped hands, but I'm in no mood and he can tell. He sits down next to me. He puts his hand on my knee. You're not going?

I'm sick.

How sick?

Bad enough.

He rubs at his stubble. What if I find the place? You want me to make the decision myself?

I don't think it will happen.

And if it does?

You know you'll never move me there.

He scowls. He checks the clock. He leaves.

Ana Iris is working her second job, so I spend my evening alone, listening to this whole country going cold on the radio. I try to keep still, but by nine I have the things he stores in my closet spread before me, the things he tells me never to touch. His books and some of his clothes, an old pair of glasses in a cardboard case, and two beaten chancletas. Hundreds of dead lottery tickets, crimped together in thick wads that fall apart at the touch. Dozens of baseball cards, Dominican players, Guzmán, Fernández, the Alous, swatting balls, winding up and fielding hard line drives just beyond the baseline. He has left me some of his dirties to wash, but I haven't had the time, and tonight I lay them out, the yeast still strong on the cuffs of his pants and work shirts.

In a box on the top shelf of the closet he has a stack of Virta's letters, cinched in a fat brown rubber band. Nearly eight years' worth. Each envelope is worn and frail and I think he's forgotten they're here. I found them a month after he stored his things, right at the start of our relationship, couldn't resist, and afterward I wished I had.

He claims that he stopped writing to her the year before, but that's not true. Every month I drop by his apartment with his laundry and read the new letters she has sent, the ones he stashes under his bed. I know Virta's name, her address, I know she works at a chocolate factory; I know that he hasn't told her about me.

The letters have grown beautiful over the years and now the handwriting has changed as well—each letter loops down, drooping into the next line like a rudder. *Please, please, mi querido husband, tell me what it is. How long did it take before your wife stopped mattering?*

After reading her letters I always feel better. I don't think this says good things about me.

WE ARE NOT HERE for fun, Ana Iris told me the day we met, and I said, Yes, you're right, even though I did not want to admit it.

Today I say these same things to Samantha and she looks at me with hatred. This morning when I arrived at the job I found her in the bathroom crying and I wish I could let her rest for an hour but we don't have those kinds of bosses. I put her on the folding and now her hands are shaking and she looks like she's going to cry again. I watch her for a long time and then I ask her what's wrong and she says, What isn't wrong?

This, Ana Iris said, is not an easy country. A lot of girls don't make it through their first year.

You need to concentrate on work, I tell Samantha. It helps.

She nods, her little girl's face vacant. It is probably her son she misses, or the father. Or our whole country, which you never think of until it's gone, which you never love until you're no longer there. I squeeze her arm and go upstairs to report in and when I come back she's gone. The other girls pretend not to notice. I check the bathroom, find a bunch of crumpled-up paper towels on the floor. I smooth them out and put them on the edge of the sink.

Even after lunch I keep expecting her to walk in and say, Here I am. I just went for a stroll.

THE TRUTH IS I am lucky to have a friend like Ana Iris. She's like my sister. Most of the people I know in the States have no friends here; they're crowded together in apartments. They're cold, they're lonely, they're worn. I've seen the lines at the phone places, the men who sell stolen card numbers, the cuarto they carry in their pockets.

When I first reached the States I was like that, alone, living over a bar with nine other women. At night no one could go to bed because of the screams and the exploding bottles from downstairs. Most of my housemates were fighting with each other over who owed who what or who had stolen money. When I myself had extra I went to the phones and called my mother, just so I could hear the voices of the people in my barrio as they passed the phone from hand to hand, like I was good luck. I was working for Ramón at that time; we weren't going out yet—that wouldn't happen for another two years. He had a housekeeping guiso then, mostly in Piscataway. The day we met he looked at me critically. Which pueblo are you from?

Moca.

Mata dictador, he said, and then a little while later he asked me which team I supported.

Águilas, I told him, not really caring.

Licey, he boomed. The only real team on the Island.

That was the same voice he used to tell me to swab a toilet or scrub an oven. I didn't like him then; he was too arrogant and too loud and I took to humming when I heard him discussing fees with the owners of the houses. But at least he didn't try to rape you like many of the other bosses. At least there was that. He kept his eyes and his hands mostly to himself. He had other plans, important plans, he told us, and just watching him you could believe it.

My first months were housecleaning and listening to Ramón argue. My first months were taking long walks through the city and waiting for Sunday to call my mother. During the day I stood in front of mirrors in those great houses and told myself that I'd done well and afterward I would come home and fold up in front of the small television we crowded around and I believed this was enough.

I met Ana Iris after Ramón's business failed. Not enough ricos around here, he said without discouragement. Some friends set up the meeting and I met her at the fish market. Ana Iris was cutting and preparing fish as we spoke. I thought she was a boricua, but later she told me she was half boricua and half dominicana. The best of the Caribbean and the worst, she said. She had fast, accurate hands and her fillets were not ragged as were some of the others on the bed of crushed ice. Can you work at a hospital? she wanted to know.

I can do anything, I said.

There'll be blood.

If you can do that, I can work in a hospital.

She was the one who took the first pictures that I mailed home, weak fotos of me grinning, well dressed and uncertain. One in front of the McDonald's, because I knew my mother would appreciate how American it was. Another one in a bookstore. I'm pretending to read, even though the book is in English. My hair is pinned up and the skin behind my ears looks pale and underused. I'm so skinny I look sick. The best picture is of me in front of a building at the university. There are no students but hundreds of metal folding chairs have been arranged in front of the building for an event and I'm facing those chairs and they're facing me and in the light my hands are startling on the blue fabric of my dress.

THREE NIGHTS A WEEK we look at houses. The houses are in terrible condition; they are homes for ghosts and for cockroaches and for us, los hispanos. Even so, few people will sell to us. They treat us well enough in person but in the end we never hear from them, and the next time Ramón drives by other people are living there, usually blanquitos, tending the lawn that should have been ours, scaring crows out of our mulberry trees. Today a grandfather, with red tints in his gray hair, tells us he likes us. He served in our country during the Guerra Civil. Nice people, he says. Beautiful people. The house is not entirely a ruin and we're both nervous. Ramón stalks about like a cat searching for a place to whelp. He steps into closets and bangs against walls and spends close to five minutes running his finger around the basement's wet seams. He smells the air for a hint of mold. In the bathroom I flush the toilet while he holds his hand under the full torrent of the shower. We both search the kitchen cabinets for roaches. In the next room the grandfather calls our references and laughs at something somebody has said.

He hangs up and says something to Ramón that I don't understand. With these people I cannot even rely on their voices. The blancos will call your mother a puta in the same voice they greet you with. I wait without hoping until Ramón leans close and tells me it looks good.

That's wonderful, I say, still sure Ramón will change his mind. He trusts very little. Out in the car he starts in, certain the old man is trying to trick him.

Why? Did you see anything wrong?

They make it look good. That's part of the trick. You watch, in two weeks the roof will start falling in.

Won't he fix it?

He says he will, but would you trust an old man like that? I'm surprised that viejo can still get around.

We say nothing more. He screws his head down into his shoulders and the cords in his neck pop out. I know he will yell if I talk. He stops at the house, the tires sliding on the snow.

Do you work tonight? I ask.

Of course I do.

He settles back into the Buick, tired. The windshield is streaked and sooty and the margins that the wipers cannot reach have a crust of dirt on them. We watch two kids pound a third with snowballs and I feel Ramón sadden and I know he's thinking about his son and right then I want to put my arm around him, tell him it will be fine.

Will you be coming by?

Depends on how the work goes.

OK, I say.

My housemates trade phony smiles over the greasy table-cloth when I tell them about the house. Sounds like you're going to be bien cómoda, Marisol says.

No worries for you.

None at all. You should be proud.

Yes, I say.

Later I lie in bed and listen to the trucks outside, their beds rattling with salt and sand. In the middle of the night I wake up and realize that he has not returned but not until morning am I angry. Ana Iris's bed is made, the netting folded neatly at its foot, a gauze. I hear her gargling in the bathroom. My hands and feet are blue from the cold and I cannot see through the window for the frost and icicles. When Ana Iris starts praying, I say, Please, just not today.

She lowers her hands. I dress.

HE'S TALKING AGAIN about the man who fell from the rafters. What would you do if that was me? he asks once more.

I would find another man, I tell him.

He smiles. Would you? Where would you find one?

You have friends, don't you?

What man would touch a dead man's novia?

I don't know, I said. I wouldn't have to tell anyone. I could find a man the way I found you.

They would be able to tell. Even the most bruto would see the death in your eyes.

A person doesn't mourn forever.

Some do. He kisses me. I bet you would. I am a hard man to replace. They tell me so at work.

How long did you mourn for your son?

He stops kissing me. Enriquillo. I mourned him a long time. I am still missing him.

I couldn't tell that by looking at you.

You don't look carefully enough.

It doesn't show, I don't think.

He puts his hand down at his side. You are not a clever woman.

I'm just saying it doesn't show.

I can see that now, he says. You are not a clever woman.

While he sits by the window and smokes I pull the last letter his wife wrote him out of my purse and open it in front of him. He doesn't know how brazen I can be. One sheet, smelling of violet water. *Please,* Virta has written neatly in the center of the page. That's all. I smile at Ramón and place the letter back in the envelope.

Ana Iris once asked me if I loved him and I told her about the lights in my old home in the capital, how they flickered and you never knew if they would go out or not. You put down your things and you waited and couldn't do anything really until the lights decided. This, I told her, is how I feel.

HERE IS WHAT the wife looks like. She is small with enormous hips and has the grave seriousness of a woman who will be called doña before she's forty. I suspect if we were in the same life we would not be friends.

I HOLD UP the blue hospital sheets in front of me and close my eyes, but the bloodstains float in the darkness in front of me. Can we save this one with bleach? Samantha asks. She is back, but I don't know for how much longer. I don't know why I don't fire her. Maybe because I want to give her a chance. Maybe because I want to see if she will stay or if she will go. What will this tell me? Very little, I suspect. In the bag at my feet I have his clothes and I wash them all together with the hospital things. For a day he will smell of my job, but I know that bread is stronger than blood.

I have not stopped watching for signs that he misses her. You must not think on these things, Ana Iris tells me. Keep them out of your mind. You do not want to go crazy from them.

This is how Ana Iris survives here, how she keeps from losing her mind over her children. How in part we all survive here. I've seen a picture of her three sons, three little boys tumbled out in the Jardín Japonés, near a pine tree, smiling, the smallest a saffron blur trying to shy away from the camera. I listen to her advice and on my way to and from work I concentrate on the other sleepwalkers around me, the men who sweep the streets and those who stand around in the backs of restaurants, with uncut hair, smoking cigarettes; the people in suits who stumble from the trains—a good many will stop at a lover's and that is all they will think about while they're eating their cold meals at home, while they're in bed with their spouses. I think of my mother, who kept with a married man when I was seven, a man with a handsome beard and craggy cheeks, who was so black that he was called Noche by everyone who knew him. He worked stringing wires for Codetel out in the campo but he lived in our barrio and had two children with a woman he had married in Pedernales. His wife was very pretty, and when I think of Ramón's wife I see her, in heels, flashing yards of brown leg, a woman warmer than the air around her. Una jeva buena. I do not imagine Ramón's wife as uneducated. She watches the telenovelas simply to pass the time. In her letters she mentions a child she tends who she loves almost as much as she had loved her own. In the beginning, when Ramón had not been gone long, she believed they could have another son, one like this Victor, her amorcito. *He plays baseball like you*, Virta wrote. She never mentions Enriquillo.

HERE THERE ARE CALAMITIES without end—but sometimes I can clearly see us in the future, and it is good. We will live in his house and I will cook for him and when he leaves food out on the counter I will call him a zángano. I can see myself watching him shave every morning. And at other times I see us in that house and see how one bright day (or a day like this, so cold your mind shifts every time the wind does) he will wake up and decide it's all wrong. He will wash his face and then turn to me. I'm sorry, he'll say. I have to leave now.

Samantha comes in sick with the flu; I feel like I'm dying, she says. She drags herself from task to task, she leans against the wall to rest, she doesn't eat anything, and the day after I have it, too. I pass it to Ramón; he calls me a fool for doing so. You think I can take a day off from work? he demands.

I say nothing; it will only irritate him.

He never stays angry for long. He has too many other things on his mind.

On Friday he comes by to update me on the house. The old man wants to sell to us, he says. He shows me some paperwork that I do not understand. He is excited but he is also scared. This is something I know, a place I've been.

What do you think I should do? His eyes are not watching me, they're looking out the window.

I think you should buy yourself a home. You deserve it.

He nods. I need to break him down on the price though. He takes out his cigarettes. Do you know how long I've waited for this? To own a house in this country is to begin to live.

I try to bring up Virta but he kills it, like always.

I already told you it's over, he snaps. What else do you want? A maldito corpse? You women never know how to leave things alone. You never know how to let go.

That night Ana Iris and I go to a movie. We cannot understand the English but we both like the new theater's clean rugs. Blue and pink neon stripes zag across the walls like lightning. We buy a popcorn to share and smuggle in cans of tamarind juice from the bodega. The people around us talk; we talk as well.

You're lucky to be getting out, she says. Those cueros are going to drive me crazy.

It's a little early for this but I say: I'm going to miss you, and she laughs.

You are on your way to another life. You won't have time to miss me.

Yes, I will. I'll probably be over to visit you every day.

You won't have the time.

I will if I make time. Are you trying to get rid of me?

Of course not, Yasmin. Don't be stupid.

It won't be for a while anyway. I remember what Ramón had said over and over again. Anything can happen.

We sit quietly for the rest of the movie. I have not asked her what she thinks of my move and she has not offered her opinion. We respect each other's silence about certain things, the way I never ask if she intends to send for her children someday.

I cannot tell what she will do. She has had men and they, too, have slept in our room, but she never kept any for long.

We walk back from the theater close together, careful of the shiny ice that scars the snow. The neighborhood is not safe. Boys who know only enough Spanish to curse stand together at the street corners and scowl. They cross into traffic without looking and when we pass them a fat one says, I eat pussy better than anybody in the world. Cochino, Ana Iris hisses, putting her hand on me. We pass the old apartment where I used to live, the one over the bar, and I stare up at it, trying to remember which window I used to stare out of. Come on, Ana Iris says. It's freezing.

RAMÓN MUST HAVE TOLD Virta something, because the letters stop. I guess it's true what they say: if you wait long enough everything changes.

As for the house, it takes longer than even I could have imagined. He almost walks away a half dozen times, slams phones, throws his drink against a wall and I expect it to fall away, not to happen. But then like a miracle it does.

Look, he says, holding up the paperwork. Look. He is almost pleading.

I'm truly happy for him. You did it, mi amor.

We did it, he says quietly. Now we can begin.

Then he puts his head down on the table and cries.

In December we move into the house. It's a half-ruin and only two rooms are habitable. It resembles the first place I lived when I arrived in this country. We don't have heat for the entire winter, and for a month we have to bathe from a bucket. Casa de Campo, I call the place in jest, but he doesn't take kindly to any criticism of his "niño." Not everyone can own a home, he reminds me. I saved eight years for this. He works on the house ceaselessly, raiding the abandoned properties on the block for materials. Every floorboard he reclaims, he boasts, is money saved. Despite all the trees, the neighborhood is not easy and we have to make sure to keep everything locked all the time.

For a few weeks people knock on the door, asking if the house is still for sale. Some of them are couples as hopeful as we must have looked. Ramón slams the door on them, as if afraid that they might haul him back to where they are. But when it's me I let them down softly. It's not, I say. Good luck with your search.

This is what I know: people's hopes go on forever.

The hospital begins to build another wing; three days after the cranes surround our building as if in prayer, Samantha pulls me aside. Winter has dried her out, left her with reptile hands and lips so chapped they look like they might at any moment split. I need a loan, she whispers. My mother's sick.

It is always the mother. I turn to go.

Please, she begs. We're from the same country.

This is true. We are.

Someone must have helped you sometime.

Also true.

The next day I give her eight hundred. It is half my savings. Remember this.

I will, she says.

She is so happy. Happier than I was when we moved into the house. I wish I could be as free. She sings for the rest of the shift, songs from when I was younger, Adamo and that lot. But she is still Samantha. Before we punch out she tells me, Don't wear so much lipstick. You have big enough lips as it is.

Ana Iris laughs. That girl said that to you?

Yes, she did.

Que desgraciada, she says, not without admiration.

At the end of the week, Samantha doesn't return to work. I ask around but no one knows where she lives. I don't remember her saying anything significant on her last day. She walked out as quietly as ever, drifting down toward the center of town, where she could catch her bus. I pray for her. I remember my own first year, how desperately I wanted to return home, how often I cried. I pray she stays, like I did.

A week. I wait a week and then I let her go. The girl who replaces her is quiet and fat and works without stopping or complaint. Sometimes, when I am in one of my moods, I imagine Samantha back home with her people. Back home

where it is warm. Saying, I would never go back. Not for anything. Not for anyone.

Some nights when Ramón is working on the plumbing or
sanding the floors I read the old letters and sip the rum we
store under the kitchen sink, and think of course of her, the
one from the other life.

I AM PREGNANT when the next letter finally arrives. Sent
from Ramón's old place to our new home. I pull it from the
stack of mail and stare at it. My heart is beating like it's lonely,
like there's nothing else inside of me. I want to open it but I
call Ana Iris instead; we haven't spoken in a long time. I stare
out at the bird-filled hedges while the phone rings.

I want to go for a walk, I tell her.

The buds are breaking through the tips of the branches.
When I step into the old place she kisses me and sits me down
at the kitchen table. Only two of the housemates I know; the
rest have moved on or gone home. There are new girls from
the Island. They shuffle in and out, barely look at me, exhausted
by the promises they've made. I want to advise them: no promises can survive that sea. I am showing, and Ana Iris is thin and
worn. Her hair has not been cut in months; the split ends rise
out of her thick strands like a second head of hair. She can still
smile, though, so brightly it is a wonder that she doesn't set
something alight. A woman is singing a bachata somewhere

upstairs, and her voice in the air reminds me of the size of this house, how high the ceilings are.

Here, Ana Iris says, handing me a scarf. Let's go for a walk.

I hold the letter in my hands. The day is the color of pigeons. Our feet crush the bits of snow that lie scattered here and there, crusted over with gravel and dust. We wait for the mash of cars to slow at the light and then we scuttle into the park. Our first months Ramón and I were in this park daily. Just to wind down after work, he said, but I painted my fingernails red every time. I remember the day before we first made love, how I already knew it would happen. He had only just told me about his wife and about his son. I was mulling over the information, saying nothing, letting my feet guide us. We met a group of boys playing baseball and he bullied the bat from them, cut at the air with it, sent the boys out deep. I thought he would embarrass himself, so I stood back, ready to pat his arm when he fell or when the ball dropped at his feet, but he connected with a sharp crack of the aluminum bat and sent the ball out beyond the children with an easy motion of his upper body. The children threw their hands up and yelled and he smiled at me over their heads.

We walk the length of the park without talking and then we head back across the highway, toward downtown.

She's writing again, I say, but Ana Iris interrupts me.

I've been calling my children, she says. She points out the man across from the courthouse, who sells her stolen calling-card numbers. They've gotten so much older, she tells me, that it's hard for me to recognize their voices.

We have to sit down after a while so that I can hold her hand and she can cry. I should say something but I don't know where a person can start. She will bring them or she will go. That much has changed.

It gets cold. We go home. We embrace at the door for what feels like an hour.

That night I give Ramón the letter and I try to smile while he reads it.

Flaca

YOUR LEFT EYE USED TO drift when you were tired or upset. It's looking for something, you used to say and those days we saw each other it fluttered and rolled and you had to put your finger over it to stop it. You were doing this when I woke up and found you on the edge of my chair. You were still in your teacher's gear but your jacket was off and enough buttons were open on your blouse to show me the black bra I bought you and the freckles on your chest. We didn't know it was the last days but we should have.

I just got here, you said and I looked out where you'd parked your Civic.

Go roll up them windows.

I'm not going to be here long.

Someone's going to steal it.

I'm almost ready to go.

You stayed in your chair and I knew better than to move closer. You had an elaborate system that you thought would keep us out of bed: you sat on the other side of the room, you didn't let me crack your knuckles, you never stayed more than fifteen minutes. It never really worked, did it?

I brought you guys dinner, you said. I was making lasagna for my class so I brought the leftovers.

My room is hot and small, overrun by books. You never wanted to be in here (it's like being inside a sock, you said) and anytime the boys were away we slept in the living room, out on the rug.

Your long hair was making you sweat and finally you took your hand away from your eye. You hadn't stopped talking.

Today I was given a new student. Her mother told me to be careful with her because she had the sight.

The sight?

You nod. I asked the señora if the sight helped her in school. She said, Not really but it's helped me with the numbers a few times.

I'm supposed to laugh but I stare outside, where a mitten-shaped leaf had stuck to your windshield. You stand beside me. When I saw you, first in our Joyce class and then at the gym, I knew I'd call you Flaca. If you'd been Dominican my family would have worried about you, brought plates of food to my door. Heaps of plátanos and yuca, smothered in liver or queso frito. *Flaca.* Even though your name was Veronica, Veronica Hardrada.

The boys will be home soon, I say. Maybe you should roll up your windows.

I'm going now, you say and put your hand back over your eye.

IT WASN'T SUPPOSED to get serious between us. I can't see us getting married or nothing and you nodded your head and said you understood. Then we fucked so that we could pretend that nothing hurtful had just happened. This was like our fifth time together and you got dressed in a black sheath and a pair of Mexican sandals and you said I could call you when I wanted but that you wouldn't call me. You have to decide where and when, you said. If you leave it up to me I'll want to see you every day.

At least you were honest, which is more than I can say for me. Weekdays I never called you, didn't even miss you. I had the boys and my job at Transactions Press to keep me busy. But Friday and Saturday nights, when I didn't meet anybody at the clubs, I called. We talked until the silences were long, until finally you asked, Do you want to see me?

I'd say yes and while I waited for you I'd tell the boys it's just sex, you know, nothing at all. And you'd come, with a change of clothes and a pan so you could make us breakfast, maybe cookies you baked for your class. The boys would find you in the kitchen the next morning, in one of my shirts and at first they didn't complain, because they guessed you would just go away. And by the time they started saying something, it was late, wasn't it?

I REMEMBER: THE BOYS keeping an eye on me. They figured two years ain't no small thing, even though the entire time I never claimed you. But what was nuts was that I felt fine. I felt like summer had taken me over. I told the boys this was the best decision I'd ever made. You can't be fucking with white-girls all your life.

In some groups that was more than a given; in our group it was not.

In that Joyce class you never spoke but I did, all the time, and once you looked at me and I looked at you and you turned so red even the professor noticed. You were whitetrash from outside of Paterson and it showed in your no-fashion-sense and you'd dated niggers a lot. I said you had a thing about us and you said, angry, No, I do not.

But you sort of did. You were the whitegirl who danced ba-chata, who pledged the SLUs, who'd gone to Santo Domingo three times already.

I remember: you used to offer me rides home in your Civic.

I remember: the third time I accepted. Our hands touched in between our seats. You tried to talk to me in Spanish and I told you to stop.

We're on speaking terms today. I say, Maybe we should go hang out with the boys, and you shake your head. I want to spend time with you, you say. If we're still good, next week maybe.

That's the most we can hope for. Nothing thrown, nothing said that we might remember for years. You watch me while you put a brush through your hair. Each strand that breaks is as long as my arm. You don't want to let go, but don't want to be hurt, either. It's not a great place to be but what can I tell you?

We drive up to Montclair, almost alone on the Parkway. Everything's quiet and dark and the trees shine from yesterday's rains. At one point, just south of the Oranges, the Parkway passes through a cemetery. Thousands of gravestones and cenotaphs on both sides. Imagine, you say, pointing to the nearest home, if you had to live in that place.

The dreams you'd have, I say.

You nod. The nightmares.

We park across from the map dealer and go to our bookstore. Despite the proximity of the college, we're the only customers, us and a three-legged cat. You sit yourself down in an aisle and start searching through the boxes. The cat goes right for you. I flip through the histories. You're the only person I've ever met who can stand a bookstore as long as I can. A smartypants, the kind you don't find every day. When I come back to you again you have kicked off your shoes and are picking at the running calluses on your feet, reading a children's book. I put my arms around your shoulders. Flaca, I say. Your hair drifts up and clings to my stubble. I don't shave often enough for anybody.

This can work, you say. We just have to let it.

THAT LAST SUMMER you wanted to go somewhere so I took us out to Spruce Run; we'd both been there as children. You could remember the years, even the months of your visits, but the closest I came was Back When I Was Young.

Look at the Queen Anne's lace, you said. You were leaning out the window into the night air and I had my hand on your back just in case.

We were both drunk and you had nothing but garters and stockings on under your skirt and you put my hand between your legs.

What did your family do here? you asked.

I looked at the night water. We had barbecues. Dominican barbecues. My pops didn't know how to but he insisted. He would cook up this red sauce that he'd splatter on chuletas and then he'd invite complete strangers over to eat. It was terrible.

I wore an eye patch when I was kid, you said. Maybe we met out here and fell in love over bad barbecue.

I doubt it, I said.

I'm just saying, Yunior.

Maybe five thousand years ago we were together.

Five thousand years ago I was in Denmark.

That's true. And half of me was in Africa.

Doing what?

Farming, I guess. That's what everybody does everywhere.

Maybe we were together some other time.

I can't think when, I said.

You tried not to look at me. Maybe five million years ago.

People weren't even people back then.

That night you lay in bed, awake, and listened to the ambulances tear down our street. The heat of your face could have kept my room warm for days. I didn't know how you stood the heat of yourself, of your breasts, of your face. I almost couldn't touch you. Out of nowhere you said, I love you. For whatever it's worth.

THAT WAS THE SUMMER I couldn't sleep, the summer I used to run through the streets of New Brunswick at four in the morning. These were the only times I broke five miles, when there was no traffic and the halogens turned everything the color of foil, firing up every bit of moisture that was on the cars. I remember running around the Memorial Homes, along Joyce Kilmer, past Throop, where the Camelot, that crazy old bar, stands boarded and burned.

I stayed up entire nights and when the Old Man came home from UPS I was writing down the times that the trains arrived from Princeton Junction—you could hear them braking from our living room, a gnash just south of my heart. I figured this staying up meant something. Maybe it was *loss* or *love* or some other word that we say when it's too fucking late but the boys weren't into melodrama. They heard that shit and said no. Especially the Old Man. Divorced at twenty, with two kids down in D.C., neither of which he sees anymore. He heard me and said, Listen. There are forty-four ways to get over this. He showed me his bitten-up hands.

WE WENT BACK to Spruce Run once more. Do you remember? When the fights seemed to go on and on and always ended with us in bed, tearing at each other like maybe that could change everything. In a couple of months you'd be seeing somebody else and I would too; she was no darker than you but she washed her panties in the shower and had hair like a sea of little puños and the first time you saw us you turned around and boarded a bus I knew you didn't have to take. When my girl said, Who was that? I said, Just some girl.

That second trip I stood on the beach and watched you wade out, watched you rub the lake on your skinny arms and neck. Both of us were hungover and I didn't want any of me wet. There's a cure in the waters, you explained. The priest announced it at service. You were saving some in a bottle. For your cousin with leukemia and your aunt with the bad heart.

You had on a bikini bottom and a T-shirt and there was a mist sifting down over the hills and lacing the trees. You went out to your waist and stopped. I was staring at you and you were staring at me and right then it was sort of like love, wasn't it?

That night you came into my bed, too thin to be believed, and when I tried to kiss your nipples you put a hand across my chest. Wait, you said.

Downstairs, the boys were watching TV, screaming.

You let the water dribble out of your mouth and it was cold. You reached my knee before you had to refill from the bottle. I listened to your breathing, how slight it was, listened to the sound the water made in the bottle. And then you covered my face and my crotch and my back.

You whispered my full name and we fell asleep in each other's arms and I remember how the next morning you were gone, completely gone, and nothing in my bed or the house could have proven otherwise.

The
Pura
Principle

THOSE LAST MONTHS. No way of wrapping it pretty or pretending otherwise: Rafa was dying. By then it was only me and Mami taking care of him and we didn't know what the fuck to do, what the fuck to say. So we just said nothing. My mom wasn't the effusive type anyway, had one of those event-horizon personalities—shit just fell into her and you never really knew how she felt about it. She just seemed to take it, never gave anything off, not light, not heat. Me, I wouldn't have wanted to talk about it even if she had been game. The few times my boys at school tried to bring it up, I told them to mind their own fucking business. To get out of my face.

I was seventeen and a half, smoking so much bud that if I remembered an hour from any one of those days it would have been a lot.

My mother was checked out in her own way. She wore herself down—between my brother and the factory and taking care of the household I'm not sure she slept. (I didn't lift a fucking finger in our apartment, male privilege, baby.) Lady *still* managed to scrounge a couple hours here and there to hang with her new main man, Jehovah. I had my yerba, she had hers. She'd never been big on church before, but as soon

as we landed on cancer planet she went so over-the-top Jesu-
cristo that I think she would have nailed herself to a cross if
she'd had one handy. That last year she was especially Ave
Maria. Had her prayer group over to our apartment two, three
times a day. The Four Horsefaces of the Apocalypse, I called
them. The youngest and the most horsefaced was Gladys—
diagnosed with breast cancer the year before, and right in the
middle of her treatment her evil husband had run off to
Colombia and married one of her cousins. Hallelujah! Another
lady, whose name I could never remember, was only forty-five
but looked ninety, a complete ghettowreck: overweight, with a
bad back, bad kidneys, bad knees, diabetes, and maybe sciatica.
Hallelujah! The chief rocker, though, was Doña Rosie, our
upstairs neighbor, this real nice boricua lady, happiest person
you've ever seen even though she was blind. Hallelujah! You
had to be careful with her because she had a habit of sitting
down without even checking if there was anything remotely
chairlike underneath her, and twice already she'd missed the
couch and busted her ass—the last time hollering, Dios mío,
qué me has hecho?—and I had to drag myself out of the basement to help her to her feet. These viejas were my mother's
only friends—even our relatives had gotten scarce after year
two—and when they were over was the only time Mami
seemed somewhat like her old self. Loved to tell her stupid
campo jokes. Wouldn't serve them coffee until she was sure
each tacita contained the exact same amount. And when one

of the Four was fooling herself she let her know it with a simple extended *Bueeeeennnnooooo*. The rest of the time, she was beyond inscrutable, in perpetual motion: cleaning, organizing, cooking meals, going to the store to return this, pick up that. The few occasions I saw her pause she would put a hand over her eyes and that was when I knew she was exhausted.

But of all of us Rafa took the cake. When he'd come home from the hospital this second go-round, he fronted like nothing had happened. Which was kinda nuts, considering that half the time he didn't know where the fuck he was because of what the radiation had done to his brain and the other half he was too tired to even fart. Dude had lost eighty pounds to the chemo, looked like a break-dancing ghoul (my brother was the last motherfucker in the Jerz to give up his tracksuit and rope chain), had a back laced with spinal-tap scars, but his swagger was more or less where it had been before the illness: a hundred percent loco. He prided himself on being the neighborhood lunatic, wasn't going to let a little thing like cancer get in the way of his official duties. Not a week out of the hospital, he cracked this illegal Peruvian kid in the face with a hammer and two hours later threw down at the Pathmark because he thought some fool was talking shit about him, popped said fool in the piehole with a weak overhand right before a bunch of us could break it up. What the fuck, he kept yelling, as if we were doing the craziest thing ever. The bruises he gave himself fighting us were purple buzz saws, infant hurricanes.

Dude was figureando *hard*. Had always been a papi chulo, so of course he dove right back into the grip of his old sucias, snuck them down into the basement whether my mother was home or not. Once, right in the middle of one of Mami's prayer sessions, he strolled in with this Parkwood girl who had the hugest donkey on the planet, and later I said, Rafa, un chín de respeto. He shrugged. Can't let them think I'm slipping. He'd hang out at Honda Hill and come home so garbled that he sounded as if he was speaking Aramaic. Anybody who didn't know better would have thought homeboy was on the mend. I'll put the weight back on, you'll see, was what he told folks. Had my mother making him all these nasty protein shakes.

Mami tried to keep his ass home. Remember what your doctor said, hijo. But he just said, Ta to, Mom, ta to, and danced right out the door. She never could control him. With me she yelled and cursed and hit, but with him she sounded as if she was auditioning for a role in a Mexican novela. Ay mi hijito, ay mi tesoro. I was all focused on this little whitegirl in Cheesequake but I tried to get him to slow his roll, too—Yo, shouldn't you be convalescing or something?—but he just stared at me with his dead eyes.

Anyway, after a few weeks on overdrive motherfucker hit a wall. Developed this dynamite cough from being out all night and ended up back at the hospital for two days—which after his last stint (eight months) didn't really count as nothing—and when he got out you could see the change. Stopped breaking night and drinking until he puked. Stopped with the Iceberg Slim thing, too. No more chicks crying over him on the couch or gobbling the rabo downstairs. The only one who hung tough was this ex of his, Tammy Franco, whom he'd pretty much physically abused their whole relationship. Bad, too. A two-year-long public-service announcement. He'd get so mad at her sometimes that he dragged her around the parking lot by her hair. Once her pants came unbuttoned and got yanked down to her ankles, and we could all see her toto and everything. That was the image I still had of her. After my brother, she had hopped on a whiteboy and gotten married faster than you can say I do. A beautiful girl. You remember that José Chinga jam "Fly Tetas"? That was Tammy. Married and beautiful and still after my brother. What was strange was that on the days she dropped by she wouldn't come into the apartment, not at all. She'd pull her Camry up in front and he would go out and sit with her in the bitch seat. I'd just started summer vacation and while I waited for the whitegirl to answer my phone calls, I'd watch them from the kitchen window, waiting for him to palm her head down into his lap, but nothing like that ever happened. It didn't even look like they were talking. After fifteen, twenty minutes, he'd climb out and she'd drive away and that would be that.

What the fuck you guys doing? Trading brain waves?

He was fingering his molars—the radiation had cost him two already.

Ain't she, like, married to some Polack? Doesn't she have, like, two kids?

He looked at me. What the fuck do you know?

Nothing.

Nothing at all. Entonces cállate la fucking boca.

So this was where he should have been from the start: taking it easy, hanging around the crib, smoking all my weed (I had to hide my puffing, while he twisted his joints right in the living room), watching the tube, sleeping. Mami was ecstatic. She even beamed every now and then. Told her group that Dios Santísimo had answered her prayers.

Alabanza, Doña Rosie said, her eyes rolling around like marbles.

I sat with him sometimes when the Mets were playing, and he wouldn't say a word about how he was feeling, what he was expecting to happen. It was only when he was in bed, dizzy or nauseous, that I'd hear him groaning: What the hell is happening? What do I do? What do I do?

I SHOULD HAVE KNOWN it was the calm before the storm. Not two weeks after he recovered from the cough, he disappeared for almost the whole day, then rolled into the apartment and announced that he had scored himself a part-time job.

A part-time job? I asked. Are you fucking nuts?

A man has to stay busy. He grinned, showed us all the gaps. Got to make myself useful.

It was at the Yarn Barn, of all places. At first my mom pretended to wash her hands of him. You want to kill yourself, kill yourself. But later I heard her trying to talk to him in the kitchen, a low monotonous appeal until my brother said: Ma, how about you leave me alone, yeah?

Talk about a total mystery. Wasn't like my brother had some incredible work ethic that needed exercising. The only job Rafa had ever had was pumping to the Old Bridge whitekids, and even on that front he'd been super chill. If he wanted to keep busy he could have gone back to that—it would have been easy, and I told him so. We still knew a lot of whitekids over in Cliffwood Beach and Laurence Harbor, a whole dirtbag clientele, but he wouldn't do it. What kind of legacy is that?

Legacy? I couldn't believe what I was hearing. Bro, you're working at the Yarn Barn!

Better than being a dealer. Anybody can do that.

And selling yarn? That's only for the giants?

He put his hands on his lap. Stared at them. You live your life, Yunior. I'll live mine.

My brother had never been the most rational of agents, but this one was the ill zinger. I chalked it up to boredom, to those eight months he had spent in the hospital. To the medicine he was taking. Maybe he just wanted to feel normal. In all honesty, he seemed pretty excited about the whole thing. Dressed up to go to the job, delicately combed that once great head of hair that had grown back sparse and pubic after the chemo. Gave himself plenty of time, too. Can't be late. Every time he headed out, my mother would slam the door behind him, and if the Hallelujah Crew was available they'd all be at their rosaries. I might have been zooted out of my gourd most of the time or chasing that girl over in Cheesequake, but I still managed to drop in on him a few times just to be sure he wasn't facedown in the mohair aisle. A surreal sight. The hardest dude in the nabe chasing price checks like a herb. I never stayed longer than it took to confirm that he was still alive. He pretended not to see me; I pretended not to have been seen.

When he brought home his first check, he threw the money on the table and laughed: I'm making bank, baby.

Oh yeah, I said, you're killing it.

Still, later that night I asked him for twenty. He looked at me and then gave it over. I jumped in the car and drove out to where Laura was supposed to be hanging with some friends but by the time I arrived she was gone.

THAT JOB NONSENSE DIDN'T LAST. I mean, how could it? After about three weeks of making the fat white ladies nervous with his skeletal self, he started forgetting shit, getting disoriented, handing customers the wrong change, cursing people out. And finally he just sat down in the middle of an aisle and couldn't get up. Too sick to drive himself home, so the job people called the apartment, got me right out of bed. I found him sitting in the office, his head hanging, and when I helped him to his feet this Spanish girl who was taking care of him started bawling as if I was leading him off to the gas chamber. He had a fever like a motherfucker. I could feel the heat through the denim of his apron.

Jesus, Rafa, I said.

He didn't lift his eyes. Mumbled, Nos fuimos.

He stretched out on the back seat of his Monarch while I drove us home. I feel like I'm dying, he said.

You ain't dying. But if you do kick it leave me the ride, OK?

I'm not leaving this baby to nobody. I'm going to be buried in it.

In this piece of crap?

Yup. With my TV and my boxing gloves.

What, you a pharaoh now?

He raised his thumb in the air. Bury your slave ass in the trunk.

The fever lasted two days, but it took a week before he was close to better, before he was spending more time on the couch than in bed. I was convinced that as soon as he was mobile he was going to head right back to the Yarn Barn or try to join the Marines or something. My mother feared the same. Told him every chance she got that it wasn't going to happen. I won't allow it. Her eyes were shining behind her black Madres de Plaza de Mayo glasses. I won't. Me, your mother, will not allow it.

Leave me alone, Ma. Leave me alone.

You could tell he was going to pull something stupid. The good thing was he didn't try to go back to the Barn.

The bad thing was that he went and basically got married.

REMEMBER THE SPANISH CHICK, the one who'd been crying over him at the Yarn Barn? Well, turns out she was actually Dominican. Not Dominican like my brother or me but *Dominican* Dominican. As in fresh-off-the-boat-didn't-have-no-papers Dominican. And thick as fucking shit. Before Rafa was even better, she started coming around, all solicitous and eager; would sit with him on the couch and watch Telemundo. (I don't have a TV, she announced at least twenty times.) Lived in London Terrace, too, over in Building 22, with her little son, Adrian, stuck in a tiny room she was renting from this older Gujarati guy, so it wasn't exactly a hardship for her to hang out with (as she put it) her gente. Even though she was trying to be all proper, keeping her legs crossed, calling my mother Señora, Rafa was on her like an octopus. By visit five, he was taking her down to the basement, whether the Hallelujah Crew was around or not.

Pura was her name. Pura Adames.

Pura Mierda was what Mami called her.

OK, for the record, I didn't think Pura was so bad; she was a hell of a lot better than most of the ho's my brother had brought around. Guapísima as hell: tall and indiecita, with huge feet and an incredibly soulful face, but unlike your average hood hottie Pura seemed not to know what to do with her fineness, was sincerely lost in all the pulchritude. A total campesina, from the way she held herself down to the way she talked, which was so demotic I couldn't understand half of what she said—she used words like *deguabinao* and *estribao* on the regular. She'd talk your ear off if you let her, and was way too honest: within a week she'd told us her whole life story. How her father had died when she was young; how for an undisclosed sum her mother had married her off at thirteen to a stingy fifty-year-old (which was how she got her first son, Nestor); how after a couple years of that terribleness she got the chance to jump from Las Matas de Farfán to Newark, brought over by a tía who wanted her to take care of her retarded son and bedridden husband; how she had run away from her, too, because she hadn't come to Nueba Yol to be a slave to anyone, not anymore; how she had spent the next four years more or less being blown along on the winds of necessity, passing through Newark, Elizabeth, Paterson, Union City, Perth Amboy (where some crazy cubano knocked her up with her second son, Adrian), everybody taking advantage of her good nature; and now here she was in London Terrace, trying to stay afloat, looking for her next break. She smiled brightly at my brother when she said that.

They don't really marry girls off like that in the DR, do they, Ma?

Por favor, Mami said. Don't believe anything that puta tells you. But a week later she and the Horsefaces were lamenting how often that happened in the campo, how Mami herself had had to fight to keep her own crazy mother from trading her for a pair of goats.

NOW, MY MOTHER, she had a simple policy when it came to my brother's "amiguitas": since none of them were ever going to last, she didn't even bother to learn their names, paid them no more heed than she'd paid our cats back in the DR. Mami wasn't mean to them or anything. If a girl said hi, she would say hi back, and if a girl was courteous Mami would return the courtesy. But the vieja didn't expend more than a watt of herself. She was unwaveringly, punishingly indifferent.

Pura, man, was another story. Right from the beginning it was clear that Mami did not like this girl. It wasn't just that Pura was mad obvious, dropping hints nonstop about her immigration status—how her life would be so much better, how her son's life would be so much better, how she would finally be able to visit her poor mother and her other son in

Las Matas, if only she had papers. Mami had dealt with paper bitches before, and she never got this pissy. Something about Pura's face, her timing, her personality, just drove Mami batshit. Felt real personal. Or maybe Mami had a presentiment of what was to come.

Whatever it was, my mother was super evil to Pura. If she wasn't getting on her about the way she talked, the way she dressed, how she ate (with her mouth open), how she walked, about her campesina-ness, about her prieta-ness, Mami would pretend that she was invisible, would walk right through her, pushing her aside, ignoring her most basic questions. If she had to refer to Pura at all, it was to say something like Rafa, what would Puta like to eat? Even I was like Jesus, Ma, what the fuck. But what made it all the iller was that Pura seemed completely oblivious of the hostility! No matter how Mami acted or what Mami said, Pura kept trying to chat Mami up. Instead of shrinking Pura, Mami's bitchiness seemed only to make her more present. When she and Rafa were alone, Pura was pretty quiet, but when Mami was around, homegirl had an opinion about *everything*, jumped in on every conversation, said shit that made no sense—like that the capital of the United States was NYC or that there were only three continents—and then would defend it to the death. You'd think with Mami stalking her she'd be careful and restrained, but nope. The girl took liberties! Búscame algo para comer, she'd say to me. No please or nothing. If I didn't get her what she wanted, she would help herself to sodas or flan. My mother would take food out of Pura's hands, but as soon as Mami turned around Pura would be back in the fridge helping herself. Even told Mami that she should paint the apartment. You need color in here. Esta sala está muerta.

I shouldn't laugh, but it was all kinda funny.

And the Horsefaces? They could have moderated things a little, don't you think, but they were, like, Fuck that, what are friendships for if not for instigating? They beat the anti-Pura drums daily. Ella es prieta. Ella es fea. Ella dejó un hijo en Santo Domingo. Ella tiene otro aquí. No tiene hombre. No tiene dinero. No tiene papeles. Qué tú crees que ella busca por aquí? They menaced Mami with the scenario of Pura getting pregnant with my brother's citizen sperm and Mami having to support her and her kids and her people in Santo Domingo *forever*, and Mami, the same woman who now prayed to God on a Mecca timetable, told the Horsefaces that if that happened she'd cut the baby out of Pura herself.

Ten mucho cuidado, she said to my brother. I don't want a mono in this house.

Too late, Rafa said, eyeing me.

My brother could have made life easier by not having Pura over so much or by limiting her to when Mami was at the factory, but when had he ever done the reasonable thing? He'd sit on the couch in the middle of all that tension, and he actually seemed to be enjoying himself.

Did he like her as much as he was claiming? Hard to say. He was definitely more caballero with Pura than he'd been with his other girls. Opening doors. Talking all polite. Even making nice with her cross-eyed boy. A lot of his ex-girls would have died to see this Rafa. This was the Rafa they'd all been waiting for.

Romeo or not, I still didn't think the relationship was going to last. I mean, my brother never kept a girl, ever; dude had thrown away better bitches than Pura on the regular.

And that was the way it seemed to go. After a month or so, Pura just disappeared. My mom didn't celebrate or anything but she wasn't unhappy, either. A couple weeks after that, though, my brother disappeared. Took the Monarch and vanished. Gone for one day, gone for two. By then Mami was starting to flip seriously out. Had the Four Horsefaces putting out an APB on the godline. I was starting to worry, too, remembering that when he was first diagnosed he'd jumped into his ride and tried to drive to Miami, where he had some boy or another. He hadn't made it past Philly before his car broke down. I got worried enough that I walked over to Tammy Franco's house, but when her Polack husband answered the door I lost my nerve. I turned around and walked away.

On the third night we were in the apartment just waiting when the Monarch pulled up. My mother ran over to the window. Holding the curtains until her knuckles were white. He's here, she said finally.

Rafa stomped in with Pura in tow. He was clearly drunk, and Pura was dressed as if they'd just been at a club.

Welcome home, Mami said quietly.

Check it out, Rafa said, holding out both his and Pura's hands.

They had rings on.

We got married!

It's official, Pura said giddily, pulling the license from her purse.

My mother went from annoyed-relieved to utterly unreadable.

Is she pregnant? she asked.

Not yet, Pura said.

Is she pregnant? My mother looked straight at my brother.

No, Rafa said.

Let's have a drink, my brother said.

My mother said: No one is drinking in my house.

I'm having a drink. My brother walked toward the kitchen but my mother stiff-armed him.

Ma, Rafa said.

No one is drinking in this house. She pushed Rafa back. If this—she threw her hand in Pura's direction—is how you want to spend the rest of your life, then, Rafael Urbano, I have nothing more to say to you. Please, I would like you and your puta to leave my house.

My brother's eyes went flat. I ain't going anywhere.

I want you both out of here.

For a second I thought my brother was going to put his hands on her. I really did. But then all the swolt went out of him. He put his arm around Pura (who, for once, looked as if she understood that something was wrong). I'll see you later, Ma, he said. Then he got back into the Monarch and drove away.

Lock the door, was all she said before she went back to her room.

I NEVER WOULD HAVE GUESSED it would last as long as it did. My mother couldn't resist my brother. Not ever. No matter what the fuck he pulled—and my brother pulled a lot of shit—she was always a hundred percent on his side, as only a Latin mom can be with her querido oldest hijo. If he'd come home one day and said, Hey, Ma, I exterminated half the planet, I'm sure she would have defended his ass: Well, hijo, we were over-populated. There was the cultural stuff, and the cancer stuff, of course, but you also got to factor in that Mami had miscarried her first two pregnancies and by the time she'd gotten knocked up with Rafa she'd been told for years she'd never have children again; my brother himself almost died at birth, and for the first two years of his life Mami had this morbid fear (so my tías tell me) that someone was going to kidnap him. Factor in, too, that he had always been the most beautiful of boys—her total consentido—and you begin to get a sense of how she felt about the lunatic. You hear mothers say all the time that they would die for their children, but my mom never said shit like that. She didn't have to. When it came to my brother, it was written across her face in 112-point Tupac Gothic.

So yeah, I figured that after a few days she'd crack, and then there'd be hugs and kisses (maybe a kick to Pura's head), and it would be all love again. But my mother wasn't playing, and she told him as much the next time Rafa came to the door.

I don't want you in here. Mami shook her head firmly. Go live with your *wife*.

You think I was surprised? You should have seen my brother. He looked shitsmacked. Fuck you then, he said to Mami, and when I told him not to talk to my mom like that he said, Fuck you, too.

Rafa, come on, I said, following him into the street. You can't be serious—you don't even know that chick.

He wasn't listening. When I got close to him, he punched me in the chest.

Hope you like the smell of Hindu, I called after him. And baby shit.

Ma, I said. What are you thinking?

Ask him what *he* is thinking.

Two days later, when Mami was at work and I was in Old Bridge hanging out with Laura—which amounted to listening to her talking about how much she hated her stepmother—

Rafa let himself into the house and grabbed the rest of his stuff. He also helped himself to his bed, to the TV, and to Mami's bed. The neighbors who saw him told us he had some Indian guy helping him. I was so mad I wanted to call the cops, but my mother forbade it. If that's how he wants to live his life, I won't stop him.

Sounds great, Ma, but what the fuck am I going to watch my shows on?

She looked at me grimly. We have another TV.

We did. A ten-inch black-and-white with its volume control permanently locked at 2.

Mami told me to bring down a spare mattress from Doña Rosie's apartment. This is just terrible what's happening, Doña Rosie said. It's nothing, Mami said. You should have seen what we slept on when I was little.

Next time I saw my brother on the street he was with Pura and the kid, looking awful in gear that no longer fit him. I yelled, You asshole, you got Mami sleeping on the fucking floor!

Don't talk to me, Yunior, he warned. I'll fucking cut your throat.

Any time, brother, I said. Any time. Now that he weighed a hundred and ten pounds and I had bench-pressed my way up to a hundred and seventy-nine, I could be aguajero, but he just ran his finger across his neck.

Leave him alone, Pura pleaded, trying to keep him from coming after me. Leave us all alone.

Oh, hi, Pura. They ain't deported you yet?

By then my brother was charging, and, a hundred and ten pounds or not, I decided not to push it. I scrammed.

Never would have predicted it, but Mami hung tough. Went to work. Did her prayer group, spent the rest of her time in her room. He's made his choice. But she didn't stop praying for him. I heard her in the group asking God to protect him, to heal him, to give him the power of discernment. Sometimes she sent me over to check up on him under the pretense of bringing him medicine. I was scared, thinking he was going to murder me on the stoop, but my mother insisted. You'll survive, she said.

First I had to be let into the apartment by the Gujarati guy, and then I had to knock and be let into their room. Pura actually kept the place pretty tight, got herself dolled up for these visits, put her son in his FOB best. She really played it to the hilt. Gave me a big hug. How are you doing, hermanito? Rafa, on the other hand, didn't seem to give two shits. He lay on the bed in his underwear, didn't say anything to me, while I sat with Pura on the edge of the bed, dutifully explaining some pill or another, and Pura would nod and nod but not look like she was getting any of it.

And then quietly I'd ask, Has he been eating? Has he been sick at all?

Pura glanced at my brother. He's been muy fuerte.

No vomiting? No fevers?

Pura shook her head.

OK, then. I got up. Bye, Rafa.

Bye, dickhole.

Doña Rosie was always with my mother when I returned from these missions, to keep Mami from seeming desperate. How did he look? la Doña asked. Did he say anything?

He called me a dickhole. I'd say that was promising.

Once, when Mami and I were heading to the Pathmark, we caught sight of my brother in the distance with Pura and the brat. I turned to watch them to see if they would wave, but my mother kept walking.

SEPTEMBER BROUGHT SCHOOL BACK. And Laura, the white-girl I'd been chasing and giving free weed, disappeared back into her regular friends. She said hi in the halls of course but she suddenly had no more time for me. My boys thought it was *hilarious*. Guess you ain't the one. Guess I ain't, I said.

Officially it was my senior year but even that seemed doubt-ful. I'd already been demoted from honors to college prep—which was Cedar Ridge's not-going-to-college track—and all I did was read, and when I was too high to read I stared out the windows.

After a couple weeks of that bullshit, I went back to cutting classes, which was the reason I'd been dumped out of honors in the first place. My mom left for work early, got back late, and couldn't read a word of English, so it wasn't as if I was ever in danger of being caught. Which was why I was home the day my brother unlocked the front door and walked into the apartment. He jumped when he saw me sitting on the couch.

What the hell are you doing here?

I laughed. What the hell are *you* doing here?

He looked awful. He had this black cold sore at the corner of his mouth, and his eyes had sunk into his face.

What the fuck you been doing to yourself? You look *terrible.*

He ignored me and went into Mami's room. I stayed seated, heard him rummaging around for a while, and then he walked out.

This happened two more times. It wasn't until the third time he was crashing around Mami's room that it dawned on my Cheech and Chong ass what was happening. Rafa was taking the money my mother kept stashed in her room! It was in a little metal box whose location she often changed but which I kept track of just in case I ever needed some bucks on the quick.

I went into her room while Rafa was mucking around in the closet, and slid the box out from one of her drawers, put it snug under my arm.

He came out of the closet. He looked at me, I looked at him. Give it to me, he said.

You ain't getting shit.

He grabbed me. Any other time of our lives this would have been no contest—he would have broken me in four—but the rules had changed. I couldn't decide which was greater: the exhilaration of beating him at something physical for the first time in my life or the fear of the same.

We knocked this over and that over, but I kept the box from him and finally he let go. I was ready for a second round, but he was shaking.

That's fine, he panted. You keep the money. But don't you worry. I'll fix you soon enough, Mr. Big Shit.

I'm terrified, I said.

That night I told Mami everything. (Of course, I stressed that it had all gone down *after* I got home from school.)

She turned the stove on under the beans she had left soaking that morning. Please don't fight your brother. Let him take whatever he wants.

But he's stealing our money!

He can have it.

Fuck that, I said. I'm going to change the lock.

No, you are not. This is his apartment, too.

Are you fucking kidding me, Ma? I was about to explode, but then it hit me.

Ma?

Yes, hijo.

How long has he been doing it?

Doing what?

Taking the money.

She turned her back to me, so I put the little metal box on the floor and went out for a smoke.

AT THE BEGINNING of October, we got a call from Pura. He's not feeling well. My mother nodded, and so I went over to check. Talk about an understatement. My brother was straight delusional. Burning up with fever and when I put my hands on him, he looked at me with zero recognition. Pura was sitting on the edge of the bed, holding her son, trying to look all worried. Give me the damn keys, I said, but she smiled weakly. We lost them.

She was lying, of course. She knew that if I got the keys to the Monarch she'd never see that car again.

He couldn't walk. He could barely move his lips. I tried to carry him but I couldn't do it, not for ten blocks, and first time ever in the history of our nabe there was no one around. By then Rafa had stopped making any kind of sense and I started getting really scared. For real: I started flipping. I thought: He's going to die here. Then I spotted a shopping cart. I dragged him over to it and put him in. We good, I said to him. We great. Pura watched us from the front stoop. I have to take care of Adrian, she explained.

All Mami's praying must have paid off, because we got one miracle that day. Guess who was parked in front of the apartment, who came running when she saw what I had in the shopping cart, who took Rafa and me and Mami and all the Horsefaces up to Beth Israel?

That's right: Tammy Franco. Aka Fly Tetas.

HE WAS IN for a long long time. A lot happened during and after, but there were no more girls. That part of his life was over. Every now and then Tammy visited him at the hospital, but it was like their old routine; she would just sit there and say nothing and he would say nothing and after a while she would leave. What the fuck is that? I asked my brother, but he never explained it, never said a word.

As for Pura—who visited my brother exactly never while he was in the hospital—she dropped by our apartment one more time. Rafa was still in Beth Israel, so I wasn't under any obligation to let her ass in, but it seemed stupid not to. Pura sat down on the couch and tried to hold my mother's hands, but Mami wasn't having any of it. She had Adrian with her, and the little manganzón immediately started running around and knocking into things, and I had to resist the urge to break my foot off in his ass. Without losing her poor-me look, Pura explained that Rafa had borrowed money from her and she needed it back; otherwise, she was going to lose her apartment.

Oh, por favor, I spat.

My mother eyed her carefully. How much was it?

Two thousand dollars.

Two thousand dollars. In 198—. This bitch was tripping.

My mother nodded thoughtfully. What do you think he did with the money?

I don't *know*, Pura whispered. He never explained *anything* to me.

And then she fucking smiled.

The girl really was a genius. Mami and I both looked like creamed shit, but she sat there as fine as anything and confident to the max—now that the whole thing was over she didn't even bother hiding it. I would have clapped if I'd had the strength, but I was too depressed.

Mami said nothing for a while, and then she went into her bedroom. I figured she was going to emerge with my father's Saturday-night special, the one thing of his that she'd kept when he left. To protect us, she claimed, but more likely to shoot my father dead if she ever saw him again. I watched Pura's kid, happily throwing around the *TV Guide*. I wondered how much he was going to like being an orphan. And then my mother came out, with a hundred-dollar bill in hand.

Ma, I said weakly.

She gave the bill to Pura but didn't let go of her end. For a minute they stared at each other, and then Mami let the bill go, the force between them so strong the paper popped.

Que Dios te bendiga, Pura said, fixing her top across her breasts before standing.

None of us saw Pura or her son or our car or our TV or our beds or the X amount of dollars Rafa had stolen for her ever again. She blew out of the Terrace sometime before Christmas to points unknown. The Gujarati guy told me when I ran into him at the Pathmark. He was still pissed because Pura had stiffed him almost two months' rent.

Last time I ever rent to one of you people.

Amen, I said.

SO YOU'D HAVE thought Rafa would be at least a little contrite, when he finally got out. Fat chance. He didn't say a thing about Pura. Didn't talk much about anything. I think he knew in a real way that he wasn't going to get better. He watched a lot of TV and sometimes he took slow walks down to the landfill. He took to wearing a crucifix, but he refused to pray or to give thanks to Jesus, as my mother asked him to. The Horsefaces were back in the apartment almost every day, and my brother would look at them and for kicks say, Fuck Jesu, and that would only get them to pray harder.

I tried to stay out of his way. I had finally hooked up with this girl who wasn't half as fine as Laura, but who at least liked me. She had introduced me to mushrooms and that was how

I was spending the time I was supposed to be in school, shrooming my ass off with her. I was so not thinking about the future.

Every now and then when me and Rafa were alone and the game was on I tried to talk to him, but he never said nothing back. His hair was all gone and he wore a Yankee cap even indoors.

And then about a month after he got out of the hospital I was coming home from the store with a gallon of milk, high and thinking about the new girl, when out of nowhere my face *exploded*. All the circuits in my brain went lights out. No idea how long I was down, but a dream and a half later I found myself on my knees, my face ablaze, holding in my hands not the milk but a huge Yale padlock.

Wasn't until I made it home and Mami put a compress on the knot under my cheek that I figured it out. Someone had thrown that lock at me. Someone who, when he was still play-ing baseball for our high school, had had his fastball clocked at ninety-three miles per hour.

That's just terrible, Rafa clucked. They could have taken your eye out.

Later, when Mami went to bed, he looked at me evenly: Didn't I tell you I was going to fix you? Didn't I?

And then he laughed.

Invierno

FROM THE TOP OF WESTMINSTER, our main strip, you could see the thinnest sliver of ocean cresting the horizon to the east. My father had been shown that sight—the management showed everyone—but as he drove us in from JFK he didn't stop to point it out. The ocean might have made us feel better, considering what else there was to see. London Terrace itself was a mess; half the buildings still needed their wiring and in the evening light these structures sprawled about like ships of brick that had run aground. Mud followed gravel everywhere and the grass, planted late in fall, poked out of the snow in dead tufts.

Each building has its own laundry room, Papi explained. Mami looked vaguely out of the snout of her parka and nodded. That's wonderful, she said. I was watching the snow sift over itself, terrified, and my brother was cracking his knuckles. This was our first day in the States. The world was frozen solid.

Our apartment seemed huge to us. Rafa and I had a room to ourselves and the kitchen, with its refrigerator and stove, was about the size of our house on Sumner Welles. We didn't stop shivering until Papi set the apartment temperature to about eighty. Beads of water gathered on the windows like bees and we had to wipe the glass to see outside. Rafa and I were stylish in our new clothes and we wanted out, but Papi told us to take off our boots and our parkas. He sat us down in front of the television, his arms lean and surprisingly hairy right up to the short-cut sleeves. He had just shown us how to flush the toilets, run the sinks, and start the shower.

This isn't a slum, Papi began. I want you to treat everything around you with respect. I don't want you throwing any of your garbage on the floor or on the street. I don't want you going to the bathroom in the bushes.

Rafa nudged me. In Santo Domingo I'd pissed everywhere, and the first time Papi had seen me in action, whizzing on a street corner, on the night of his triumphant return, he had screamed, What in carajo are you doing?

Decent people live around here and that's how we're going to live. You're Americans now. He had his Chivas Regal bottle on his knee.

After waiting a few seconds to show that yes, I'd digested everything he'd said, I asked, Can we go out now?

Why don't you help me unpack? Mami suggested. Her hands were very still; usually they were fussing with a piece of paper, a sleeve, or each other.

We'll just be out for a little while, I said. I got up and pulled on my boots. Had I known my father even a little I might not have turned my back on him. But I didn't know him; he'd spent the last five years in the States working, and we'd spent the last five years in Santo Domingo waiting. He grabbed my ear and wrenched me back onto the couch. He did not look happy.

You'll go out when I say you're ready.

I looked over at Rafa, who sat quietly in front of the TV. Back on the Island, the two of us had taken guaguas clear across the capital by ourselves. I looked up at Papi, his narrow face still unfamiliar. Don't you eye me, he said.

Mami stood up. You kids might as well give me a hand.

I didn't move. On the TV the newscasters were making small, flat noises at each other. They were repeating one word over and over. Later when I went to school I would learn that the word they were saying was *Vietnam*.

SINCE WE WEREN'T ALLOWED out of the house—it's too cold, Papi said once but really there was no reason other than that's what he wanted—we mostly sat in front of the TV or stared out at the snow those first days. Mami cleaned everything about ten times and made us some damn elaborate lunches. We were all bored speechless.

Pretty early on Mami decided that watching TV was beneficial; you could learn the language from it. She saw our young minds as bright, spiky sunflowers in need of light, and arranged us as close to the TV as possible to maximize our exposure. We watched the news, sitcoms, cartoons, *Tarzan, Flash Gordon, Jonny Quest, The Herculoids, Sesame Street*—eight, nine hours of

TV a day, but it was *Sesame Street* that gave us our best lessons. Each word my brother and I learned we passed between ourselves, repeating over and over, and when Mami asked us to show her how to say it, we shook our heads and said, Don't worry about it.

Just tell me, she said, and when we pronounced the words slowly, forming huge, lazy soap bubbles of sound, she never could duplicate them. Her lips seemed to tug apart even the simplest vowels. That sounds horrible, I said.

What do you know about English? she asked.

At dinner she'd try her English out on Papi, but he just poked at his pernil, which was not my mother's best dish.

I can't understand a word you're saying, he said finally. It's best if I take care of the English.

How do you expect me to learn?

You don't have to learn, he said. Besides, the average woman can't learn English.

It's a difficult language to master, he said, first in Spanish and then in English.

Mami didn't say another word. In the morning, as soon as Papi was out of the apartment, Mami turned on the TV and put us in front of it. The apartment was always cold in the morning and leaving our beds was a serious torment.

It's too early, we said.

It's like school, she suggested.

No, it's not, we said. We were used to going to school at noon.

You two complain too much. She would stand behind us and when I turned around she would be mouthing the words we were learning, trying to make sense of them.

EVEN PAPI'S EARLY-MORNING noises were strange to me. I lay in bed, listening to him stumbling around in the bathroom, like he was drunk or something. I didn't know what he did for Reynolds Aluminum, but he had a lot of uniforms in his closet, all filthy with machine oil.

I had expected a different father, one about seven feet tall with enough money to buy our entire barrio, but this one was average height, with an average face. He'd come to our house in Santo Domingo in a busted-up taxi and the gifts he had brought us were small things—toy guns and tops—that we were too old for, that we broke right away. Even though he hugged us and took us out to dinner on the Malecón—our first steaks ever—I didn't know what to make of him. A father is a hard thing to compass.

Those first weeks in the States, Papi spent a great deal of his home time downstairs with his books or in front of the TV. He said little to us that wasn't disciplinary, which didn't surprise us. We'd seen other dads in action, understood that part of the drill.

INVIERNO

My brother he just tried to keep from yelling, from knocking things over. But what he got on me about the most was my shoelaces. Papi had a thing with shoelaces. I didn't know how to tie them properly, and when I put together a rather formidable knot, Papi would bend down and pull it apart with one tug. At least you have a future as a magician, Rafa said, but this was serious. Rafa showed me how, and I said, Fine, and had no problems in front of him, but when Papi was breathing down my neck, his hand on a belt, I couldn't perform; I looked at my father like my laces were live wires he wanted me to touch together.

I met some dumb men in the Guardia, Papi said, but every single one of them could tie his motherfucking shoes. He looked over at Mami. Why can't he?

These were not the sort of questions that had answers. She looked down, studied the veins that threaded the backs of her hands. For a second Papi's watery turtle eyes met mine. Don't you look at me, he said.

Even on days I managed a halfway decent retard knot, as Rafa called them, Papi still had my hair to go on about. While Rafa's hair was straight and glided through a comb like a Caribbean grandparent's dream, my hair still had enough of the African to condemn me to endless combings and out-of-this-world haircuts. My mother cut our hair every month, but this time when she put me in the chair my father told her not to bother.

Only one thing will take care of that, he said. You, go get dressed.

Rafa followed me into my bedroom and watched while I buttoned my shirt. His mouth was tight. I started to feel anxious. What's your problem? I said.

Nothing.

Then stop watching me. When I got to my shoes, he tied them for me. At the door my father looked down and said, You're getting better.

I knew where the van was parked but I went the other way just to catch a glimpse of the neighborhood. Papi didn't notice my defection until I had rounded the corner, and when he growled my name I hurried back, but I had already seen the fields and the children on the snow.

I sat in the front seat. He popped a tape of Johnny Ventura into the player and took us out smoothly to Route 9. The snow lay in dirty piles on the side of the road. There can't be anything worse than old snow, he said. It's nice while it falls but once it gets to the ground it just turns to shit.

Are there accidents like with rain?

Not with me driving.

The cattails on the banks of the Raritan were stiff and the color of sand, and when we crossed the river, Papi said, I work in the next town.

We were in Perth Amboy for the services of a real talent, a Puerto Rican barber named Rubio who knew just what to do with the pelo malo. He put two or three creams on my head and had me sit with the foam awhile; after his wife rinsed me off he studied my head in the mirror, tugged at my hair, rubbed an oil into it, and finally sighed.

It's better to shave it all off, Papi said.

I have some other things that might work.

Papi looked at his watch. Shave it.

All right, Rubio said. I watched the clippers plow through my hair, watched my scalp appear, tender and defenseless. One of the old men in the waiting area snorted and held his paper higher. I was sick to my stomach; I didn't want him to shave it but what could I have said to my father? I didn't have the words. When Rubio was finished he massaged talcum powder on my neck. Now you look guapo, he said, less than convinced. He handed me a stick of gum, which my brother would steal as soon as I got home.

Well? Papi asked.

You cut too much, I said truthfully.

It's better like this, he said, paying the barber.

As soon as we were outside the cold clamped down on my head like a slab of wet dirt.

We drove back in silence. An oil tanker was pulling into port on the Raritan and I wondered how easy it would be for me to slip aboard and disappear.

Do you like negras? my father asked.

I turned my head to look at the women we had just passed. I turned back and realized that he was waiting for an answer, that he wanted to know, and while I wanted to blurt that I didn't like girls in any denomination, I said instead, Oh yes, and he smiled.

They're beautiful, he said, and lit a cigarette. They'll take care of you better than anyone.

Rafa laughed when he saw me. You look like a big thumb.

Dios mío, Mami said, turning me around. Why did you do that to him?

It looks good, Papi said.

And the cold's going to make him sick.

Papi put his cold palm on my head. He likes it fine, he said.

PAPI WORKED A LONG fifty-hour week and on his days off he expected quiet, but my brother and I had too much energy to be quiet; we didn't think anything of using our sofas for trampolines at nine in the morning, while Papi was asleep. In our old barrio we were accustomed to folks shocking the streets with merengue twenty-four hours a day. Our upstairs neighbors, who themselves fought like trolls over everything, would stomp down on us. Will you two please shut up? and then Papi would come out of his room, his shorts unbuttoned, and say, What did I tell you? How many times have I told you to keep it quiet? He was free with his smacks and we spent whole afternoons on Punishment Row—our bedroom—where we had to lay on our beds and not get off, because if he burst in and caught us at the window, staring out at the beautiful snow, he would pull our ears and smack us, and then we would have to kneel in the corner for a few hours. If we messed that up, joking around or cheating, he would force us to kneel down on the cutting side of a coconut grater, and only when we were bleeding and whimpering would he let us up.

Now you'll be quiet, he'd say, satisfied, and we'd lay in bed, our knees burning with iodine, and wait for him to go to work so we could put our hands against the cold glass.

We watched the neighborhood children building snowmen and igloos, having snowball fights. I told my brother about the field I'd seen, vast in my memory, but he just shrugged. A brother and sister lived across in apartment four, and when they were out we would wave to them. They waved to us and motioned for us to come out but we shook our heads: We can't.

The brother tugged his sister out to where the other children were, with their shovels and their long, snow-encrusted scarves. She seemed to like Rafa, and waved to him as she walked off. He didn't wave back.

American girls are supposed to be beautiful, he said.

Have you seen any?

What do you call her? He reached down for a tissue and sneezed out a doublebarrel of snot. All of us had headaches and colds and coughs; even with the heat cranked up, winter was kicking our asses. I had to wear a Christmas hat around the apartment to keep my shaven head warm; I looked like an unhappy tropical elf.

I wiped my nose. If this is the United States, mail me home.

Don't worry. Mami says we're probably going home.

How does she know?

Her and Papi have been talking about it. She thinks it would be better if we went back. Rafa ran a finger glumly over our window; he didn't want to go; he liked the TV and the toilet and already saw himself with the girl in apartment four.

I don't know about that, I said. Papi doesn't look like he's going anywhere.

What do you know? You're just a little mojón.

I know more than you, I said. Papi had never once mentioned going back to the Island. I waited to get him in a good mood, after he had watched Abbott and Costello, and asked him if he thought we would be going back soon.

For what?

A visit.

You ain't going anywhere.

BY THE THIRD WEEK I was worried we weren't going to make it. Mami, who had been our authority on the Island, was dwindling. She cooked our food and then sat there, waiting to wash

INVIERNO

the dishes. She had no friends, no neighbors to visit. You should talk to me, she said, but we told her to wait for Papi to get home. He'll talk to you, I guaranteed. Rafa's temper got worse. I would tug at his hair, an old game of ours, and he would explode. We fought and fought and fought and after my mother pried us apart, instead of making up like the old days, we sat scowling on opposite sides of our room and planned each other's demise. I'm going to burn you alive, he promised. You should number your limbs, I told him, so they'll know how to put you back together for the funeral. We squirted acid at each other with our eyes, like reptiles. Our boredom made everything worse.

One day I saw the brother and sister from apartment four gearing up to go play, and instead of waving I pulled on my parka. Rafa was sitting on the couch, flipping between a Chinese cooking show and an all-star Little League game. I'm going out, I told him.

Sure you are, he said, but when I pushed open the front door, he said, Hey!

The air outside was very cold and I nearly fell down our steps. No one in the neighborhood was the shoveling type. Throwing my scarf over my mouth, I stumbled across the uneven crust of snow. I caught up to the brother and sister at the side of our building.

Wait up! I yelled. I want to play with you.

The brother watched me with a half grin, not understanding a word I'd said, his arms scrunched nervously at his sides. His hair was a frightening no-color. His sister had green eyes and her freckled face was cowled in a hood of pink fur. We had on the same brand of mittens, bought cheap from Two Guys. I stopped and we faced each other, our white breath nearly reaching across the distance between us. The world was ice and the ice burned with sunlight. This was my first real encounter with Americans and I felt loose and capable. I motioned with my mittens and smiled. The sister turned to her brother and laughed. He said something to her and then she ran to where the other children were, the peals of her laughter trailing over her shoulder like the spumes of her hot breath.

I've been meaning to come out, I said. But my father won't let us right now. He thinks we're too young, but look, I'm older than your sister, and my brother looks older than you.

The brother pointed at himself. Eric, he said.

My name's Yunior, I said.

His grin never faded. Turning, he walked over to the approaching group of children. I knew that Rafa was watching me from the window and fought the urge to turn around and wave. The gringo children watched me from a distance and then walked away. Wait, I said, but then an Oldsmobile pulled into the next lot, its tires muddy and thick with snow. I couldn't follow them. The sister looked back once, a lick of her hair peeking out of her hood. After they had gone, I stood in the snow until my feet were cold. I was too afraid of getting my ass beat to go any farther.

Rafa was sprawled in front of the TV.

Hijo de la gran puta, I said, sitting down.

You look frozen.

I didn't answer him. We watched TV until a snowball struck the glass patio door and both of us jumped.

What was that? Mami wanted to know from her room.

Two more snowballs exploded on the glass. I peeked behind the curtain and saw the brother and the sister hiding behind a snow-buried Dodge.

Nothing, Señora, Rafa said. It's just the snow.

What, is it learning how to dance out there?

It's just falling, Rafa said.

We both stood behind the curtain and watched the brother throw fast and hard, like a pitcher.

EACH DAY THE TRUCKS would roll into our neighborhood with the garbage. The landfill stood two miles out, but the mechanics of the winter air conducted its sound and odors to us undiluted. When we opened a window we could hear and smell the bulldozers spreading the garbage out in thick, putrid layers across the top of the landfill. We could see the gulls attending the mound, thousands of them, wheeling.

Do you think kids play out there? I asked Rafa. We were standing on the porch, brave; at any moment Papi could pull into the parking lot and see us.

Of course they do. Wouldn't you?

I licked my lips. They must find a lot of stuff out there.

Plenty, Rafa said.

That night I dreamed of home, that we'd never left. I woke up, my throat aching, hot with fever. I washed my face in the sink, then sat next to our window, my brother asleep, and watched the pebbles of ice falling and freezing into a shell over the cars and the snow and the pavement. Learning to sleep in new places was an ability you were supposed to lose as you grew older, but I never had it. The building was only now settling into itself; the tight magic of the just-hammered-in nail was finally relaxing. I heard someone walking around in the living room and when I went out I found my mother standing in front of the patio door.

You can't sleep? she asked, her face smooth and perfect in the glare of the halogens.

I shook my head.

We've always been alike that way, she said. That won't make your life any easier.

I put my arms around her waist. That morning alone we'd seen three moving trucks from our patio door. I'm going to pray for Dominicans, she had said, her face against the glass, but what we would end up getting were Puerto Ricans.

INVIERNO

She must have put me to bed because the next day I woke up next to Rafa. He was snoring. Papi was in the next room snoring as well, and something inside of me told me that I wasn't a quiet sleeper.

At the end of the month the bulldozers capped the landfill with a head of soft, blond dirt, and the evicted gulls flocked over the development, shitting and fussing, until the first of the new garbage was brought in.

MY BROTHER WAS BUCKING to be Number One Son; in all other things he was generally unchanged, but when it came to my father he obeyed him with a scrupulousness he had never shown anybody. My brother was usually an animal but in my father's house he had turned into some kind of muchacho bueno. Papi said he wanted us inside, Rafa stayed inside. It was as if the passage to the U.S. had burned out the sharpest part of him. In no time at all it would spark back to life more terrible than before but those first months he was muted. I don't think anybody could have recognized him. I wanted my father to like me too but I wasn't in an obedient mood; I played in the snow for short stretches, though never out of sight of the apartment. You're going to get caught, Rafa forecasted. I could tell that my boldness made him miserable; from our windows he watched me packing snow and throwing myself into drifts. I stayed away from the gringos. When I saw the brother and sister from apartment four, I stopped farting around and watched for a sneak attack. Eric waved and his sister waved; I didn't wave back. Once he came over and showed me the baseball he must have just gotten. Roberto Clemente, he said, but I went on with building my fort. His sister grew flushed and said something loud and then Eric moved off.

One day the sister was out by herself and I followed her to the field. Huge concrete pipes sprawled here and there on the snow. She ducked into one of these and I followed her, crawling on my knees.

She sat in the pipe, crosslegged and grinning. She took her hands out of her mittens and rubbed them together. We were out of the wind and I followed her example. She poked a finger at me.

Yunior, I said.

Elaine, she said.

We sat there for a while, my head aching with my desire to communicate, and she kept blowing on her hands. Then she heard her brother calling and she scrambled out of the pipe. I stepped out too. She was standing next to her brother. When he saw me he yelled something and threw a snowball in my direction. I threw one back.

In less than a year they would be gone. All the white

people would be. All that would be left would be us colored folks.

AT NIGHT, MAMI AND PAPI TALKED. He sat on his side of the table and she leaned close, asking him, Do you ever plan on taking these children out? You can't keep them sealed up like this.

They'll be going to school soon, he said, sucking on his pipe. And as soon as winter lets up I want to show you the ocean. You can see it around here, you know, but it's better to see it up close.

How much longer does winter last?

Not long, he promised. You'll see. In a few months none of you will remember this and by then I won't have to work too much. We'll be able to travel in spring and see everything.

I hope so, Mami said.

My mother was not a woman easily cowed, but in the States she let my father roll over her. If he said he had to be at work for two days straight, she said OK and cooked enough moro to last him. She was depressed and sad and missed her father and her friends, our neighbors. Everyone had warned her that the U.S. was a difficult place where even the Devil got his ass beat, but no one had told her that she would have to spend the rest of her natural life snowbound with her children. She wrote letter after letter home, begging her sisters to come as soon as possible. This neighborhood is empty and friendless. And she begged my father to bring his friends over. She wanted to talk about unimportant matters, to speak to someone who wasn't her child or her spouse.

None of you are ready for guests, Papi said. Look at this house. Look at your children. Me da vergüenza to see them slouching around like that.

You can't complain about this apartment. All I do is clean it.

What about your sons?

My mother looked over at me and then at Rafa. I put one shoe over the other. After that, she had Rafa keep after me about my shoelaces. When we heard our father's van arriving in the parking lot, Mami called us over for a quick inspection. Hair, teeth, hands, feet. If anything was wrong she'd hide us in the bathroom until it was fixed. Her dinners grew elaborate. She even changed the TV for Papi without calling him a zángano.

OK, he said finally. Maybe it can work.

It doesn't have to be anything big, Mami said.

Two Fridays in a row he brought a friend over for dinner and Mami put on her best polyester jumpsuit and got us spiffy in our red pants, thick white belts, and amaranth-blue Chams shirts. Seeing her asthmatic with excitement made us hopeful too that our world was about to change for the better, but these were awkward dinners. The men were bachelors and divided their time between talking to Papi and eyeing Mami's ass. Papi seemed to enjoy their company but Mami spent her time on her feet, hustling food to the table, opening beers, and changing the channel. She started out each night natural and unreserved, with a face that scowled as easily as it grinned, but as the men loosened their belts and aired out their toes and talked their talk, she withdrew; her expressions narrowed until all that remained was a tight, guarded smile that seemed to drift across the room the way a shadow drifts slowly across a wall. We kids were ignored for the most part, except once, when the first man, Miguel, asked, Can you two box as well as your father?

They're fine fighters, Papi said.

Your father is very fast. Has good hand speed. Miguel leaned in. I saw him finish this one gringo, beat him until he was squealing.

Miguel had brought a bottle of Bermúdez rum; he and my father were drunk.

It's time you go to your room, Mami said, touching my shoulder.

Why? I asked. All we do is sit there.

That's how I feel about my home, Miguel said.

Mami's glare cut me in half. Shut your mouth, she said, shoving us toward our room. We sat, as predicted, and listened. On both visits, the men ate their fill, congratulated Mami on her cooking, Papi on his sons, and then stayed about an hour for propriety's sake. Cigarettes, dominos, gossip, and then the inevitable, Well, I have to get going. We have work tomorrow. You know how that is.

Of course I do. What else do we Dominicans know?

Afterward, Mami cleaned the pans quietly in the kitchen, scraping at the roasted pig flesh, while Papi sat out on our front porch in his short sleeves; he seemed to have grown impervious to the cold these last five years. When he came inside, he showered and pulled on his overalls. I have to work tonight, he said.

Mami stopped scratching at the pans with a spoon. You should find yourself a more regular job.

Papi shrugged. If you think jobs are easy to find, you go get one.

As soon as he left, Mami ripped the needle from the album and interrupted Felix del Rosario. We heard her in the closet, pulling on her coat and her boots.

Do you think she's leaving us? I asked.

Rafa wrinkled his brow. Maybe, he said.

When we heard the front door open, we let ourselves out of our room and found the apartment empty.

We better go after her, I said.

Rafa stopped at the door. Let's give her a minute, he said.

What's wrong with you?

We'll wait two minutes, he said.

One, I said loudly. He pressed his face against the glass patio door. We were about to hit the door when she returned, panting, an envelope of cold around her.

Where did you go? I asked.

I went for a walk. She dropped her coat at the door; her face was red from the cold and she was breathing deeply, as if she'd sprinted the last thirty steps.

Where?

Just around the corner.

Why the hell did you do that?

She started to cry, and when Rafa put his hand on her waist, she slapped it away. We went back to our room.

I think she's losing it, I said.

She's just lonely, Rafa said.

THE NIGHT BEFORE THE SNOWSTORM I heard the wind at our window. I woke up the next morning, freezing. Mami was fiddling with the thermostat; we could hear the gurgle of water in the pipes but the apartment didn't get much warmer.

Just go play, Mami said. That will keep your mind off it.

Is it broken?

I don't know. She looked at the knob dubiously. Maybe it's slow this morning.

None of the gringos were outside playing. We sat by the window and waited for them. In the afternoon my father called from work; I could hear the forklifts when I answered.

Rafa?

No, it's me.

Get your mother.

We got a big storm on the way, he explained to her—even from where I was standing I could hear his voice. There's no way I can get out to see you. It's gonna be bad. Maybe I'll get there tomorrow.

What should I do?

Just keep indoors. And fill the tub with water.

Where are you sleeping? Mami asked.

At a friend's.

She turned her face from us. OK, she said. When she got off the phone she sat in front of the TV. She could see I was going to pester her about Papi; she told me, Just watch your show.

Radio WADO recommended spare blankets, water, flashlights, and food. We had none of these things. What happens if we get buried? I asked. Will we die? Will they have to save us in boats?

I don't know, Rafa said. I don't know anything about snow. I was spooking him. He went over to the window and peered out.

We'll be fine, Mami said. As long as we're warm. She went over and raised the heat again.

But what if we get buried?

You can't have that much snow.

How do you know?

Because twelve inches isn't going to bury anybody, even a pain in the ass like you.

I went out on the porch and watched the first snow begin to fall like finely sifted ash. If we die, Papi's going to feel bad, I said.

Mami turned away and laughed.

Four inches fell in an hour and the snow kept falling.

Mami waited until we were in bed, but I heard the door and woke Rafa. She's at it again, I said.

Outside?

Yes.

He put on his boots grimly. He paused at the door and then looked back at the empty apartment. Let's go, he said.

She was standing on the edge of the parking lot, ready to cross Westminster. The apartment lamps glared on the frozen ground and our breath was white in the night air. The snow was gusting.

Go home, she said.

We didn't move.

Did you at least lock the front door? she asked.

Rafa shook his head.

It's too cold for thieves anyway, I said.

Mami smiled and nearly slipped on the sidewalk. I'm not good at walking on this vaina.

I'm real good, I said. Just hold on to me.

We crossed Westminster. The cars were moving very slowly and the wind was loud and full of snow.

This isn't too bad, I said. These people should see a hurricane.

Where should we go? Rafa asked. He was blinking a lot to keep the snow out of his eyes.

Go straight, Mami said. That way we don't get lost.

We should mark the ice.

She put her hands around us both. It's easier if we go straight.

We went down to the edge of the apartments and looked out over the landfill, a misshapen, shadowy mound that abutted the Raritan. Rubbish fires burned all over it like sores and the dump trucks and bulldozers slept quietly and reverently at its base. It smelled like something the river had tossed out from its floor, something moist and heaving. We found the basketball courts next and the pool, empty of water, and Parkwood, the next neighborhood over, which was all moved in and full of kids.

We even saw the ocean, up there at the top of Westminster, like the blade of a long, curved knife. Mami was crying but we pretended not to notice. We threw snowballs at the sliding cars and once I removed my cap just to feel the snowflakes scatter across my cold, hard scalp.

Miss
Lora

1

Years later you would wonder if it hadn't been for your brother would you have done it? You remember how all the other guys had hated on her—how skinny she was, no culo, no titties, como un palito but your brother didn't care. I'd fuck her.

You'd fuck anything, someone jeered.

And he had given that someone the eye. You make that sound like it's a bad thing.

2

Your brother. Dead now a year and sometimes you still feel a fulgurating sadness over it even though he really was a super asshole at the end. He didn't die easy at all. Those last months he just steady kept trying to run away. They would catch him trying to hail a cab outside of Beth Israel or walking down some Newark street in his greens. Once he conned an ex-girlfriend into driving him to California but outside of Camden he started having convulsions and she called you in a panic. Was it some atavistic impulse to die alone, out of sight? Or was he just trying to fulfill something that had always been inside of him? Why are you doing that? you asked but he just laughed. Doing what?

In those last weeks when he finally became too feeble to run away he refused to talk to you or your mother. Didn't utter a single word until he died. Your mother did not care. She loved him and prayed over him and talked to him like he was still OK. But it wounded you, that stubborn silence. His last fucking days and he wouldn't say a word. You'd ask him something straight up, How are you feeling today, and Rafa would just turn his head. Like you all didn't deserve an answer. Like no one did.

3

You were at the age where you could fall in love with a girl over an expression, over a gesture. That's what happened with your girlfriend, Paloma—she stooped to pick up her purse and your heart flew out of you.

That's what happened with Miss Lora, too.

It was 1985. You were sixteen years old and you were messed up and alone like a motherfucker. You also were convinced—like totally utterly convinced—that the world was going to blow itself to pieces. Almost every night you had nightmares that made the ones the president was having in *Dreamscape* look like pussyplay. In your dreams the bombs were always going off, evaporating you while you walked, while you ate a chicken wing, while you took the bus to school, while you fucked Paloma. You would wake up biting your own tongue in terror, the blood dribbling down your chin.

Someone really should have medicated you.

Paloma thought you were being ridiculous. She didn't want to hear about Mutual Assured Destruction, *The Late Great Planet Earth*, We begin bombing in five minutes, SALT II, *The Day After, Threads, Red Dawn, WarGames, Gamma World*, any of it. She called you Mr. Depressing. And she didn't need any more depressing than she had already. She lived in a one-bedroom apartment with four younger siblings and a disabled mom and she was taking care of all of them. That and honors classes. She didn't have time for *anything* and mostly stayed with you, you suspected, because she felt bad for what had happened with your brother. It's not like you ever spent much time together or had sex or anything. Only Puerto Rican girl on the earth who wouldn't give up the ass for any reason. I can't, she said. I can't make *any mistakes*. Why is sex with me a mistake, you demanded, but she just shook her head, pulled your hand out of her pants. Paloma was convinced that if she made *any mistakes* in the next two years, *any mistakes at all*, she would be stuck in that family of hers forever. That was *her* nightmare. Imagine if I don't get in anywhere, she said. You'd still have me, you tried to reassure her, but Paloma looked at you like the apocalypse would be preferable.

So you talked about the Coming Doomsday to whoever would listen—to your history teacher, who claimed he was building a survival cabin in the Poconos, to your boy who was stationed in Panama (in those days you still wrote letters), to your around-the-corner neighbor, Miss Lora. That was what connected you two at first. She listened. Better still, she had read *Alas, Babylon* and had seen part of *The Day After*, and both had scared her monga.

The Day After wasn't scary, you complained. It was crap. You can't survive an airburst by ducking under a dashboard.

Maybe it was a miracle, she said, playing.

A miracle? That was just dumbness. What you need to see is *Threads*. Now that is some real shit.

I probably wouldn't be able to stand it, she said. And then she put her hand on your shoulder.

People always touched you. You were used to it. You were an amateur weightlifter, something else you did to keep your mind off the shit of your life. You must have had a mutant gene somewhere in the DNA, because all the lifting had turned you into a goddamn circus freak. Most of the time it didn't bother you, the way girls and sometimes guys felt you up. But with Miss Lora you could tell something was different.

Miss Lora touched you and you suddenly looked up and

noticed how large her eyes were on her thin face, how long her lashes were, how one iris had more bronze in it than the other.

4

Of course you knew her; she was your neighbor, taught over at Sayreville HS. But it was only in the past months that she snapped into focus. There were a lot of these middle-aged single types in the neighborhood, shipwrecked by every kind of catastrophe, but she was one of the few who didn't have children, who lived alone, who was still kinda young. Something must have happened, your mother speculated. In her mind a woman with no child could only be explained by vast untrammeled calamity.

Maybe she just doesn't like children.

Nobody likes children, your mother assured you. That doesn't mean you don't have them.

Miss Lora wasn't nothing exciting. There were about a thousand viejas in the neighborhood way hotter, like Mrs. del Orbe, whom your brother had fucked silly until her husband found out and moved the whole family away. Miss Lora was too skinny. Had no hips whatsoever. No breasts, either, no ass, even her hair failed to make the grade. She had her eyes, sure, but what she was most famous for in the neighborhood were her muscles. Not that she had huge ones like you—chick was just wiry like a motherfucker, every single fiber standing out in outlandish definition. Bitch made Iggy Pop look chub, and every summer she caused a serious commotion at the pool. Always a bikini despite her curvelessness, the top stretching over these corded pectorals and the bottom cupping a rippling fan of haunch muscles. Always swimming underwater, the black waves of her hair flowing behind her like a school of eel. Always tanning herself (which none of the other women did) into the deep lacquered walnut of an old shoe. That woman needs to keep her clothes on, the mothers complained. She's like a plastic bag full of worms. But who could take their eyes off her? Not you or your brother. The kids would ask her, Are you a bodybuilder, Miss Lora? and she would shake her head behind her paperback. Sorry, guys, I was just born this way.

After your brother died she came over to the apartment a couple of times. She and your mother shared a common place, La Vega, where Miss Lora had been born and where your mother had recuperated after the Guerra Civil. One full year living just behind the Casa Amarilla had made a vegana out of your mother. I still hear the Río Camú in my dreams, your mother said. Miss Lora nodded. I saw Juan Bosch once on our street when I was very young. They sat and talked about it to death. Every now and then she stopped you in the parking lot. How are you doing? How is your mother? And you never knew what to say. Your tongue was always swollen, raw, from being blown to atoms in your sleep.

5

Today you come back from a run to find her on the stoop, talking to la Doña. Your mother calls you. Say hello to the profesora.

I'm sweaty, you protest.

Your mother flares. Who in carajo do you think you're talking to? Say hello, coño, to la profesora.

Hello, profesora.

Hello, student.

She laughs and turns back to your mother's conversation.

You don't know why you're so furious all of a sudden.

I could curl you, you say to her, flexing your arm.

And Miss Lora looks at you with a ridiculous grin. What in the world are you talking about? I'm the one who could pick *you* up.

She puts her hands on your waist and pretends to make the effort.

Your mother laughs thinly. But you can feel her watching the both of you.

6

When your mother had confronted your brother about Mrs. del Orbe he didn't deny it. What do you want, Ma? Se metío por mis ojos.

Por mis ojos my ass, she had said. Tú te metiste por su culo.

That's true, your brother admitted cheerily. Y por su boca.

And then your mother punched him, helpless with shame and fury, which only made him laugh.

7

It is the first time any girl ever wanted you. And so you sit with it. Let it roll around in the channels of your mind. This is nuts, you say to yourself. And later, absently, to Paloma. She doesn't hear you. You don't really know what to do with the knowledge. You ain't your brother, who would have run right over and put a rabo in Miss Lora. Even though you know, you're scared you're wrong. You're scared she'd laugh at you.

So you try to keep your mind off her and the memory of her bikinis. You figure the bombs will fall before you get a chance to do shit. When they don't fall, you bring her up to Paloma in a last-ditch effort, tell her la profesora has been after you. It feels very convincing, that lie.

That old fucking hag? That's *disgusting*.

You're telling me, you say in a forlorn tone.

That would be like fucking a stick, she says.

It would be, you confirm.

You better not fuck her, Paloma warns you after a pause.

What are you talking about?

I'm just telling you. Don't fuck her. You know I'll find out. You're a terrible liar.

Don't be a crazy person, you say, glaring. I'm not fucking anyone. Clearly.

That night you are allowed to touch Paloma's clit with the tip of your tongue but that's it. She holds your head back with the force of her whole life and eventually you give up, demoralized.

It tasted, you write your boy in Panama, like beer.

You add an extra run to your workout, hoping it will cool your granos, but it doesn't work. You have a couple dreams where you are about to touch her but then the bomb blows NYC to kingdom come and you watch the shock wave roll up and then you wake, your tongue clamped firmly between your teeth.

And then you are coming back from Chicken Holiday with a four-piece meal, a drumstick in your mouth, and there she is walking out of Pathmark, wrestling a pair of plastic bags. You consider bolting but your brother's law holds you in place. *Never run.* A law he ultimately abrogated but which you right now cannot. You ask meekly: You want help with that, Miss Lora?

She shakes her head. It's my exercise for the day. You walk back together in silence and then she says: When are you going to come by to show me that movie?

What movie?

The one you said is the real one. The nuclear war movie.

Maybe if you were someone else you would have the discipline to duck the whole thing but you are your father's son and your brother's brother. Two days later you are home and the silence in there is terrible and it seems like the same commercial for fixing tears in your car upholstery is on. You shower, shave, dress.

I'll be back.

Your mom is looking at your dress shoes. Where are you going?

Out.

It's ten o'clock, she says, but you're already out the door.

You knock on the door once, twice, and then she opens up. She is wearing sweats and a Howard T-shirt and she tenses her forehead worriedly. Her eyes look like they belong on a giant's face.

You don't bother with the small talk. You just push up and kiss. She reaches around and shuts the door behind you.

THIS IS HOW YOU LOSE HER

Do you have a condom?

You are a worrier like that.

Nope, she says and you try to keep control but you come in her anyway.

I'm really sorry, you say.

It's OK, she whispers, her hands on your back, keeping you from pulling out. Stay.

8

Her apartment is about the neatest place you've ever seen and for its lack of Caribbean craziness could be inhabited by a white person. On her walls she has a lot of pictures of her travels and her siblings and they all seem incredibly happy and square. So you're the rebel? you ask her and she laughs. Something like that.

There are also pictures of some guys. A few you recognize from when you were younger and about them you say nothing.

She is very quiet, very reserved while she fixes you a cheeseburger. Actually, I hate my family, she says, squashing the patty down with a spatula until the grease starts popping.

You wonder if she feels like you do. Like it might be love. You put on *Threads* for her. Get ready for some real shit, you say.

Get ready for me to hide, she responds, but you two only last an hour before she reaches over and takes off your glasses and kisses you. This time your wits are back so you try to find the strength to fight her off.

I can't, you say.

And just before she pops your rabo in her mouth she says: Really?

You try to think of Paloma, so exhausted that every morning she falls asleep on the ride to school. Paloma, who still found the energy to help you study for your SAT. Paloma, who didn't give you any ass because she was terrified that if she got pregnant she wouldn't abort it out of love for you and then her life would be over. You're trying to think of her but what you're doing is holding Miss Lora's tresses like reins and urging her head to keep its wonderful rhythm.

You really do have an excellent body, you say after you blow your load.

Why, thank you. She motions with her head. You want to go into the bedroom?

Even more fotos. None of them will survive the nuclear blast, you are sure. Nor will this bedroom, whose window faces toward New York City. You tell her that. Well, we'll just have to make do, she says. She gets naked like a pro and once you start she closes her eyes and rolls her head around like it's on a broken hinge. She clasps your shoulders with a nailed grip as strong as shit and you know that after, your back is going to look like it's been whipped.

Then she kisses your chin.

9

Both your father and your brother were sucios. Shit, your father used to take you on his pussy runs, leave you in the car while he ran up into cribs to bone his girlfriends. Your brother was no better, boning girls in the bed next to yours. Sucios of the worst kind and now it's official: you are one, too. You had hoped the gene missed you, skipped a generation, but clearly you were kidding yourself. The blood always shows, you say to Paloma on the ride to school next day. Yunior, she stirs from her doze, I don't have time for your craziness, OK?

10

You figure you can keep it to a one-time thing. But the next day you go right back. You sit gloomily in her kitchen while she fixes you another cheeseburger.

Are you going to be OK? she asks.

I don't know.

It's just supposed to be fun.

I have a girlfriend.

You told me, remember?

She puts the plate on your lap, regards you critically. You know, you look like your brother. I'm sure people tell you that all the time.

Some people.

I couldn't believe how good-looking he was. He knew it, too. It was like he never heard of a shirt.

This time you don't even ask about the condom. You just come inside her. You are surprised at how pissed you are. But she kisses your face over and over and it moves you. No one has ever done that. The girls you boned, they were always ashamed afterward. And there was always panic. Someone heard. Fix the bed up. Open the windows. Here there is none of that.

Afterward, she sits up, her chest as unadorned as yours. So what else do you want to eat?

II

You try to be reasonable. You try to control yourself, to be smooth. But you're at her apartment every fucking day. The one time you try to skip, you recant and end up slipping out of your apartment at three in the morning and knocking furtively on her door until she lets you in. You know I work, right? I know, you say, but I dreamed that something happened to you. That's sweet of you to lie, she sighs and even though she is falling asleep she lets you bone her straight in the ass. Fucking amazing, you keep saying for all four seconds it takes you to come. You have to pull my hair while you do it, she confides. That makes me shoot like a rocket.

It should be the greatest thing, so why are your dreams worse? Why is there more blood in the sink in the morning?

You learn a lot about her life. She came up with a Dominican doctor father who was crazy. Her mother left them for an Italian waiter, fled to Rome, and that was it for pops. Always threatening to kill himself and at least once a day she would have to beg him not to and that had messed her up but good. In her youth she'd been a gymnast and there was even talk of making the Olympic team, but then the coach robbed the money and the DR had to cancel for that year. I'm not claiming I would have won, she says, but I could have done something. After that bullshit she put on a foot of height and that was it for gymnastics. Then her father got a job in Ann Arbor, Michigan, and she and her three little siblings went with him. After six months he moved them in with a fat widow, una blanca asquerosa who hated Lora. She had no friends at all in school and in ninth grade she slept with her high school history teacher. Ended up living in his house. His ex-wife was also a teacher at the school. You can only imagine what that was like. As soon as she graduated she ran off with a quiet black boy to a base in Ramstein, Germany, but that hadn't worked. To this day I think he was gay, she says. And finally after trying to make it in Berlin she came home. She moved in with a girlfriend who had an apartment in London Terrace, dated a few guys, one of her ex's old Air Force buddies who visited her on his leaves, a moreno with the sweetest disposition. When the girlfriend got married and moved away Miss Lora kept the apartment and got a teaching job. Made a conscious effort to stop moving. It was an OK life, she says, showing you the pictures. All things considered.

She is always trying to get you to talk about your brother. It will help, she says.

What is there to say? He got cancer, he died.

Well, that's a start.

She brings home college brochures from her school. She gives them to you with half the application filled out. You really need to get out of here.

Where? you ask her.

Go anywhere. Go to Alaska for all I care.

She sleeps with a mouth guard. And she covers her eyes with a mask.

If you have to go, wait till I fall asleep, OK? But after a few weeks it's Please don't go. And finally just: Stay.

And you do. At dawn you slip out of her apartment and into your basement window. Your mother doesn't have a fucking clue. In the old days she used to know everything. She had that campesino radar. Now she is somewhere else. Her grief, tending to it, takes all her time.

You are scared stupid at what you are doing but it is also exciting and makes you feel less lonely in the world. And you are sixteen and you have a feeling that now that the Ass Engine has started, no force on the earth will ever stop it.

Then your abuelo catches something in the DR and your mother has to fly home. You'll be fine, la Doña says. Miss Lora said she'd look after you.

I can cook, Ma.

No you can't. And don't bring that Puerto Rican girl in here. Do you understand?

You nod. You bring the Dominican woman in instead.

She squeals with delight when she sees the plastic-covered sofas and the wooden spoons hanging on the wall. You admit to feeling a little bad for your mother.

Of course you end up downstairs in your basement. Where your brother's things are still in evidence. She goes right for his boxing gloves.

Please put those down.

She pushes them into her face, smelling them.

You can't relax. You keep swearing that you hear your mother or Paloma at the door. It makes you stop every five minutes.

It's unsettling to wake up in your bed with her. She makes coffee and scrambled eggs and listens not to Radio WADO but
to the Morning Zoo and laughs at everything. It's too strange.
Paloma calls to see if you are going to school and Miss Lora is
walking around in a T-shirt, her flat skinny rump visible.

12

Then your senior year she gets a job at your high school. Of
course. To say it is strange is to say nada. You see her in the
halls and your heart goes through you. That's your neighbor?
Paloma asks. God, she's fucking looking at you. The old whore.
At the school the Spanish girls are the ones who give her trouble. They make fun of her accent, her clothes, her physique.
(They call her Miss Pat.) She never complains about it—It's a
really great job, she says—but you see the nonsense firsthand.
It's just the Spanish girls, though. The whitegirls love her to
death. She takes over the gymnastics team. She brings them to
dance programs for inspiration. And in no time at all they start
winning. One day outside the school the gymnasts are all egg-
ing her on and she does a back handspring that nearly staggers
you with its perfection. It is the most beautiful thing you ever
saw. Of course Mr. Everson, the science teacher, falls all over
her. He's always falling over someone. For a while it was Paloma

until she threatened to report his ass. You see them laughing in the hallways, you see them having lunch in the teachers' room.

Paloma doesn't stop busting. They say Mr. Everson likes to put on dresses. You think she straps it on for him?

You girls are nuts.

She probably does strap it on.

It all makes you very tense. But it does make the sex that much better.

A few times you see Mr. Everson's car outside her apartment. Looks like Mr. Everson is in the hood, one of your boys laughs. You suddenly find yourself weak with fury. You think about fucking up his car. You think about knocking on the door. You think a thousand things. But you stay at home lifting until he leaves. When she opens the door you stalk in without saying a word to her. The house reeks of cigarettes.

You smell like shit, you say.

You walk into her bedroom but the bed is made.

Ay mi pobre, she laughs. No seas celoso.

But of course you are.

13

You graduate in June and she is there with your mother, clapping. She is wearing a red dress because you once told her it was your favorite color and underneath matching underwear. Afterward she drives you both to Perth Amboy for a Mexican dinner. Paloma can't come along because her mother is sick. But you see her late that night in front of her apartment.

I did it, Paloma says, cheesing.

I'm proud of you, you say. And then you add, uncharacteristically: You are an extraordinary young woman.

That summer you and Paloma see each other maybe twice—there are no more make-out sessions. She's already gone. In August she leaves for the University of Delaware. You are not surprised when after about a week on campus she writes you a letter with the header MOVING ON. You don't even bother finishing it. You think about driving all the way down there to talk to her but you realize how hopeless that is. As might be expected, she never comes back.

You stay in the neighborhood. You land a job at Raritan River Steel. At first you have to fight the Pennsylvania hillbillies but eventually you find your footing and they leave you alone. At night you go to the bars with some of the other idiots who stuck around the neighborhood, get seriously faded, and show up at Miss Lora's door with your dick in your hand. She's still pushing the college thing, offers to pay all the admission fees but your heart ain't in it and you tell her, Not right now. She's taking night classes herself at Montclair. She's thinking of getting her Ph.D. Then you'll have to call me doctora.

Occasionally you two meet up in Perth Amboy, where

people don't know either of you. You have dinner like normal folks. You look too young for her and it kills you when she touches you in public but what can you do? She's always happy to be out with you. You know this ain't going to last, you tell her and she nods. I just want what's best for you. You try your damnedest to meet other girls, telling yourself they'll help you transition, but you never meet anyone you really like.

Sometimes after you leave her apartment you walk out to the landfill where you and your brother played as children and sit on the swings. This is also the spot where Mr. del Orbe threatened to shoot your brother in the nuts. Go ahead, Rafa said, and then my brother here will shoot *you* in the pussy. Behind you in the distance hums New York City. The world, you tell yourself, will never end.

14

It takes a long time to get over it. To get used to a life without a Secret. Even after it's behind you and you've blocked her completely, you're still afraid you'll slip back to it. At Rutgers, where you've finally landed, you date like crazy and every time it doesn't work out you're convinced that you have trouble with girls your own age. Because of her.

You certainly never talk about it. Until senior year when you meet the mujerón of your dreams, the one who leaves her moreno boyfriend to date you, who drives all your little chickies out the coop. She's the one you finally trust. The one you finally tell.

They should arrest that crazy bitch.

It wasn't like that.

They should arrest her ass today.

Still it is good to tell someone. In your heart you thought she would hate you—that they would all hate you.

I don't hate you. Tú eres mi hombre, she says proudly.

When you two visit the apartment she brings it up to your mother. Doña, es verdad que tu hijo taba rapando una vieja?

Your mother shakes her head in disgust. He's just like his father and his brother.

Dominican men, right, Doña?

These three are worse than the rest.

Afterward, she makes you walk past Miss Lora's spot. There is a light on.

I'm going to go have a word with her, the mujerón says.

Don't. Please.

I'm going to.

She bangs on the door.

Negra, please don't.

Answer the door! she yells.

No one does.

You don't speak to the mujerón for a few weeks after that.

It's one of your big breakups. But finally you're both at a Tribe Called Quest show and she sees you dancing with another girl and she waves to you and that does it. You go up to where she's seated with all her evil line sisters. She has shaved her head again.

Negra, you say.

She pulls you over to a corner. I'm sorry I got carried away. I just wanted to protect you.

You shake your head. She steps into your arms.

15

Graduation: it's not a surprise to see her there. What surprises you is that you didn't predict it. The instant before you and the mujerón join the procession you see her standing alone in a red dress. She is finally starting to put on weight; it looks good on her. Afterward, you spot her walking alone across the lawn of Old Queens, carrying a mortarboard she picked up. Your mother grabbed a second one, too. Hung it on her wall.

What happens is that in the end she moves away from London Terrace. Prices are going up. The Banglas and the Pakistanis are moving in. A few years later your mother moves, too, up to the Bergenline.

Later, after you and the mujerón are over, you will type her name into the computer but she never turns up. On one DR trip you drive up to La Vega and put her name out there. You show a picture, too, like a private eye. It is of the two of you, the one time you went to the beach, to Sandy Hook. Both of you are smiling. Both of you blinked.

The Cheater's Guide to Love

Year 0

Your girl catches you cheating. (Well, actually she's your fiancée, but hey, in a bit it *so* won't matter.) She could have caught you with one sucia, she could have caught you with two, but as you're a totally batshit cuero who didn't ever empty his e-mail trash can, she caught you with fifty! Sure, over a six-year period, but still. Fifty fucking girls? God*damn*. Maybe if you'd been engaged to a super open-minded blanquita you could have survived it—but you're not engaged to a super open-minded blanquita. Your girl is a bad-ass salcedeña who doesn't believe in open anything; in fact the one thing she warned you about, that she swore she would never forgive, was *cheating*. I'll put a machete in you, she promised. And of course you swore you wouldn't do it. You swore you wouldn't. You swore you wouldn't.

And you did.

She'll stick around for a few months because you dated for a long long time. Because you went through much together—her father's death, your tenure madness, her bar exam (passed on the third attempt). And because love, real love, is not so easily shed. Over a tortured six-month period you will fly to the DR, to Mexico (for the funeral of a friend), to New Zealand. You will walk the beach where they filmed *The Piano*, something she's always wanted to do, and now, in penitent desperation, you give it to her. She is immensely sad on that beach and she walks up and down the shining sand alone, bare feet in the freezing water, and when you try to hug her she says, *Don't*. She stares at the rocks jutting out of the water, the wind taking her hair straight back. On the ride back to the hotel, up through those wild steeps, you pick up a pair of hitchhikers, a couple, so mixed it's ridiculous, and so giddy with love that you almost throw them out the car. She says nothing. Later, in the hotel, she will cry.

You try every trick in the book to keep her. You write her letters. You drive her to work. You quote Neruda. You compose a mass e-mail disowning all your sucias. You block their e-mails. You change your phone number. You stop drinking. You stop smoking. You claim you're a sex addict and start attending meetings. You blame your father. You blame your mother. You blame the patriarchy. You blame Santo Domingo. You find a therapist. You cancel your Facebook. You give her the passwords to all your e-mail accounts. You start taking salsa classes like you always swore you would so that the two of you could dance together. You claim that you were sick, you claim that you were weak—It was the book! It was the pressure!—and every hour like clockwork you say that you're so so sorry. You try it all, but one day she will simply sit up in bed and say, *No more,* and, *Ya,* and you will have to move from the Harlem apartment that you two have shared. You consider not going. You consider a squat protest. In fact, you say won't go. But in the end you do.

For a while you haunt the city, like a two-bit ballplayer dreaming of a call-up. You phone her every day and leave messages which she doesn't answer. You write her long sensitive letters, which she returns unopened. You even show up at her apartment at odd hours and at her job downtown until finally her little sister calls you, the one who was always on your side, and she makes it plain: If you try to contact my sister again she's going to put a restraining order on you.

For some Negroes that wouldn't mean shit.

But you ain't that kind of Negro.

You stop. You move back to Boston. You never see her again.

Year 1

At first you pretend it don't matter. You harbored a lot of grievances against her anyway. Yes you did! She didn't give good head, you hated the fuzz on her cheeks, she never waxed her pussy, she never cleaned up around the apartment, etc. For a few weeks you almost believe it. Of course you go back to smoking, to drinking, you drop the therapist and the sex addict groups and you run around with the sluts like it's the good old days, like nothing has happened.

I'm back, you say to your boys.

Elvis laughs. It's almost like you never left.

You're good for like a week. Then your moods become erratic. One minute you have to stop yourself from jumping in the car and driving to see her and the next you're calling a sucia and saying, You're the one I always wanted. You start losing your temper with friends, with students, with colleagues. You cry every time you hear Monchy and Alexandra, her favorite.

Boston, where you never wanted to live, where you feel you've been exiled to, becomes a serious problem. You have trouble adjusting to it full-time; to its trains that stop running at midnight, to the glumness of its inhabitants, to its startling lack of Sichuan food. Almost on cue a lot of racist shit starts happening. Maybe it was always there, maybe you've become more sensitive after all your time in NYC. White people pull up at traffic lights and scream at you with a hideous rage, like you nearly ran over their mothers. It's fucking scary. Before you can figure out what the fuck is going on they flip you the bird and peel out. It happens again and again. Security follows you in stores and every time you step on Harvard property you're asked for ID. Three times, drunk whitedudes try to pick fights with you in different parts of the city.

You take it all very personally. I hope someone drops a fucking *bomb* on this city, you rant. This is why no people of color want to live here. Why all my black and Latino students leave as soon as they can.

Elvis says nothing. He was born and raised in Jamaica Plain, knows that trying to defend Boston from uncool is like blocking a bullet with a slice of bread. Are you OK? he asks finally.

I'm dandy, you say. Mejor que nunca.

Except you're not. You've lost all the mutual friends you had in NYC (they went to her), your mother won't speak to you after what happened (she liked the fiancée better than she liked you), and you're feeling terribly guilty and terribly alone. You keep writing letters to her, waiting for the day that you can hand them to her. You also keep fucking everything that moves. Thanksgiving you end up having to spend in your apartment because you can't face your mom and the idea of other people's charity makes you furious. The ex, as you're now calling her, always cooked: a turkey, a chicken, a pernil. Set aside all the wings for you. That night you drink yourself into a stupor, spend two days recovering.

You figure that's as bad as it gets. You figure wrong. During finals a depression rolls over you, so profound you doubt there is a name for it. It feels like you're being slowly pincered apart, atom by atom.

You stop hitting the gym or going out for drinks; you stop shaving or washing your clothes; in fact, you stop doing almost everything. Your friends begin to worry about you, and they

THE CHEATER'S GUIDE TO LOVE

are not exactly the worrying types. I'm OK, you tell them, but with each passing week the depression darkens. You try to describe it. Like someone flew a plane into your soul. Like someone flew two planes into your soul. Elvis sits shivah with you in the apartment; he pats you on the shoulder, tells you to take it easy. Four years earlier Elvis had a Humvee blow up on him on a highway outside of Baghdad. The burning wreckage pinned him for what felt like a week, so he knows a little about pain. His back and buttocks and right arm so scarred up that even you, Mr. Hard Nose, can't look at them. Breathe, he tells you. You breathe nonstop, like a marathon runner, but it doesn't help. Your little letters become more and more pathetic. *Please*, you write. *Please come back.* You have dreams where she's talking to you like in the old days—in that sweet Spanish of the Cibao, no sign of rage, of disappointment. And then you wake up.

You stop sleeping, and some night when you're drunk and alone you have a wacky impulse to open the window of your fifth-floor apartment and leap down to the street. If it wasn't for a couple of things you probably would have done it, too. But (a) you ain't the killing-yourself type; (b) your boy Elvis keeps a strong eye on you—he's over all the time, stands by the window as if he knows what you're thinking. And (c) you have this ridiculous hope that maybe one day she will forgive you.

She doesn't.

Year 2

You make it through both semesters, barely. It really is a long stretch of shit and then finally the madness begins to recede. It's like waking up from the worst fever of your life. You ain't your old self (har-har!) but you can stand near windows without being overcome by strange urges, and that's a start. Unfortunately, you've put on forty-five pounds. You don't know how it happened but it happened. Only one pair of your jeans fits anymore, and none of your suits. You put away all the old pictures of her, say good-bye to her Wonder Woman features. You go the barber, shave your head for the first time in forever and cut off your beard.

You done? Elvis asks.

I'm done.

A white grandma screams at you at a traffic light and you close your eyes until she goes away.

Find yourself another girl, Elvis advises. He's holding his daughter lightly. Clavo saca clavo.

Nothing sacas nothing, you reply. No one will ever be like her.

OK. But find yourself a girl anyway.

His daughter was born that February. If she had been a boy Elvis was going to name him Iraq, his wife told you.

I'm sure he was kidding.

She looked out to where he was working on his truck. I don't think so.

He puts his daughter in your arms. Find yourself a good Dominican girl, he says.

You hold the baby uncertainly. Your ex never wanted kids but toward the end she made you get a sperm test, just in case she decided last minute to change her mind. You put your lips against the baby's stomach and blow. Do they even exist?

You had one, didn't you?

That you did.

You CLEAN UP your act. You cut it out with all the old sucias, even the long-term Iranian girl you'd boned the entire time you were with the fiancée. You want to turn over a new leaf. Takes you a bit—after all, old sluts are the hardest habit to ditch—but you finally break clear and when you do you feel lighter. I should have done this years ago, you declare, and your girl Arlenny, who never ever messed with you (Thank God, she mutters) rolls her eyes. You wait, what, a week for the bad energy to dissipate and then you start dating. Like a normal person, you tell Elvis. Without any lies. Elvis says nothing, only smiles.

At first it's OK: you get numbers but nothing you would take home to the fam. But after the early rush, it all dries up. It ain't just a dry spell; it's fucking Arrakeen. You're out all the time but no one seems to be biting. Not even the chicks who swear they *love Latin guys*, and one girl, when you tell her you are Dominican, actually says, Hell no and runs full-tilt toward the door. Seriously? you say. You begin to wonder if there is some secret mark on your forehead. If some of these bitches *know*.

Be patient, Elvis urges. He's working for this ghetto-ass landlord and starts taking you with him on collection day. It turns out you're awesome backup. Deadbeats catch one peep of your dismal grill and cough up their debts with a quickness.

One month, two month, three month and then some hope. Her name is Noemi, Dominican from Baní—in Massachusetts it seems all the domos are from Baní—and you meet at Sofia's in the last months before it closes, fucking up the Latino community of New England forever. She ain't half your ex but she ain't bad either. She's a nurse, and when Elvis complains about his back, she starts listing all the shit it might be. She's a big girl and got skin like you wouldn't believe and best of all she doesn't privar at all; actually seems *nice*. She smiles often and whenever she's nervous she says, Tell me something. Minuses: she's always working and she has a four-year-old named Justin. She shows you pictures; kid looks like he'll be dropping an album if she's not careful. She had him with a banilejo who had four other kids with four other women. And you thought this guy was a good idea for what reason? you say. I was stupid, she admits. Where did you meet him? Same place I met you, she says. Out.

Normally that would be a no-go, but Noemi is not only nice, she's also kinda fly. One of those hot moms and you're excited for the first time in over a year. Even standing next to her while a hostess looks for menus gives you an erection.

Sunday is her one day off—the Five-Baby Father watches Justin that day, or better said, he and his new girlfriend watch Justin that day. You and Noemi fall into a little pattern: on Saturday you take her out to dinner—she doesn't eat anything remotely adventurous, so it's always Italian—and then she stays the night.

How sweet was that toto? Elvis asks after the first sleepover.

Not sweet at all, because Noemi doesn't give it to you! Three Saturdays in a row she sleeps over, and three Saturdays in a row nada. A little kissing, a little feeling up, but nothing beyond that. She brings her own pillow, one of those expensive foam ones, and her own toothbrush, and she takes it all with her Sunday morning. Kisses you at the door as she leaves; it all feels too chaste to you, too lacking in promise.

No toto? Elvis looks a little shocked.

No toto, you confirm. What am I, in sixth grade?

You know you should be patient. You know she's just testing your ass. She's probably had a lot of bad experiences with the hit-and-run types. Case in point—Justin's dad. But it galls you that she gave it up to some thug with no job, no education, no nothing, but she's making you jump through hoops of fire. In fact, it infuriates you.

Are we going to see each other? she asks on week four, and you almost say yes but then your idiocy gets the best of you.

It depends, you say.

On what? She is instantly guarded and that adds to your irritation. Where was that guard when she let the banilejo fuck her without a condom?

On whether you're planning to give me ass anytime soon.

Oh classiness. You know as soon as you say it that you just buried yourself.

Noemi is silent. Then she says: Let me get off this phone before I say something you won't like.

This is your last chance, but instead of begging for mercy you bark: *Fine.*

Within an hour she has deleted you from Facebook. You send one exploratory text to her but it is never answered.

Years later you will see her in Dudley Square but she will pretend not to recognize you, and you won't force the issue.

Nicely done, Elvis says. Bravo.

You two are watching his daughter knock around the playground near Columbia Terrace. He tries to be reassuring. She had a kid. That probably wasn't for you.

Probably not.

Even these little breakups suck because they send you right back to thinking about the ex. Right back into the depression. This time you spend six months wallowing in it before you come back to the world.

After you pull yourself back together you tell Elvis: I think I need a break from the bitches.

What are you going to do?

Focus on me for a while.

That's a good idea, says his wife. Besides it only happens when you're not looking for it.

That's what everybody claims. Easier to say that than This shit sucks.

This shit sucks, Elvis says. Does that help?

Not really.

On the walk home a Jeep roars past; the driver calls you a *fucking towelhead.* One of the ex-sucias publishes a poem about you online. It's called "El Puto."

Year 3

You take your break. You try to get back to your work, to your writing. You start three novels: one about a pelotero, one about a narco and one about a bachatero—all of them suck pipe. You get serious about classes and for your health you take up running. You used to run in the old days and you figure you need something to keep you out of your head. You must have needed it bad, because once you get into the swing of it you start running four five six times a week. It's your new addiction. You run in the morning and you run late at night when there's no one on the paths next to the Charles. You run so hard that your heart feels like it's going to seize. When winter rolls in, there's a part of you that fears you'll fold—Boston winters are on some terrorism shit—but you need the activity more than anything so you keep at it even as the trees are stripped of their foliage and the paths empty out and the frost reaches into your bones. Soon it's only you and a couple of other lunatics. Your body changes, of course. You lose all that drinking and smoking chub and your legs look like they belong to someone else. Every time you think about the ex, every time the loneliness rears up in you like a seething, burning continent, you tie on your shoes and hit the paths and that helps; it really does.

By winter's end you've gotten to know all the morning regulars and there's even this one girl who inspires in you some hope. You pass each other a couple of times a week and she's a pleasure to watch, a gazelle really—what economy, what gait, and what an amazing fucking cuerpazo. She has Latin features but your radar has been off a while and she could just as likely be a morena as anything. She always smiles at you as you pass. You consider flopping in front of her—My leg! My leg!—but that seems incredibly cursí. You keep hoping you'll bump into her around town.

The running is going splendid and then six months in you feel a pain in your right foot. Along the inside arch, a burning that doesn't subside after a few days' rest. Soon you're hobbling even when you're not running. You drop in on emergency care and the RN pushes with his thumb, watches you writhe, and announces you have plantar fasciitis.

You have no idea what that is. When can I run again?

He gives you a pamphlet. Sometimes it takes a month. Sometimes six months. Sometimes a year. He pauses. Sometimes longer.

That makes you so sad you go home and lie in bed in the dark. You're afraid. I don't want to go back down the hole, you tell Elvis. Then don't, he says. Like a hardhead you keep trying to run but the pain sharpens. Finally, you give up. You put away the shoes. You sleep in. When you see other people hitting the paths, you turn away. You find yourself crying in front of sporting goods stores. Out of nowhere you call the ex, but of course she doesn't pick up. The fact that she hasn't changed her number gives you some strange hope, even though you've heard she's dating somebody. Word on the street is that the dude is super good to her.

Elvis encourages you to try yoga, the half-Bikram kind they teach in Central Square. Mad fucking ho's in there, he says. I'm talking ho's by the ton. While you're not exactly feeling the ho's right now, you don't want to lose all the conditioning you've built up, so you give it a shot. The namaste bullshit you could do without, but you fall into it and soon you're pulling vinyasas with the best of them. Elvis was certainly right. There are mad ho's, all with their asses in the air, but none of them catch your eye. One miniature blanquita does try to chat you up. She seems impressed that of all the guys in class you alone never take off your shirt, but you skitter away from her cornpoke grin. What the hell are you going to do with a blanquita?

Bone the shit out of her, Elvis offers.

Bust a nut in her mouth, your boy Darnell seconds.

Give her a chance, Arlenny proposes.

But you don't do any of it. At the end of the sessions you move away quickly to wipe down your mat and she takes the hint. She doesn't mess with you again, though sometimes during practice she watches you with longing.

You actually become pretty obsessed with yoga and soon you're taking your mat with you wherever you go. You no longer have fantasies that the ex will be waiting for you in front of your apartment, though every now and then you still call her and let the phone ring to the in-box.

You finally start work on your eighties apocalypse novel—"finally starting" means you write one paragraph—and in a flush of confidence you start messing with this young morena from the Harvard Law School that you meet at the Enormous Room. She's half your age, one of those super geniuses who finished undergrad when she was nineteen and is seriously lovely. Elvis and Darnell approve. Aces, they say. Arlenny demurs. She's really young, no? Yes, she's really young and you fuck a whole lot and during the act the two of you cling to each other for dear life but afterward you peel away like you're ashamed of yourselves. Most of the time you suspect she feels sorry for you. She says she likes your mind, but considering that she's smarter than you, that seems doubtful. What she does appear to like is your body, can't keep her hands off it. I should get back to ballet, she says while undressing you. Then you'd lose your thick, you note, and she laughs. I know, that's the dilemma.

It's all going swell, going marvelous, and then in the middle of a sun salutation you feel a shift in your lower back and *pau*—it's like a sudden power failure. You lose all strength, have to lie down. Yes, urges the instructor, rest if you have to. When the class is over you need help from the little whitegirl to rise to your feet. Do you want me to take you somewhere? she asks but you shake your head. The walk back to your apartment is some Bataan-type shit. At the Plough and Stars you fall against a stop sign and call Elvis on your cell.

He arrives in a flash with a hottie in tow. She's a straight-up Cambridge Cape Verdean. The two of them look like they've just been fucking. Who's that? you ask and he shakes his head. Drags you into emergency care. By the time the doctor appears you're crabbed over like an old man.

It appears to be a ruptured disc, she announces.

Yay, you say.

You're in bed for a solid two weeks. Elvis brings you food and sits with you while you eat. He talks about the Cape

Verdean girl. She's got like the perfect pussy, he says. It's like putting your dick in a hot mango.

You listen for a bit and then you say: Just don't end up like me.

Elvis grins. Shit, no one could ever end up like you, Yunior. You're a DR original.

His daughter throws your books onto the floor. You don't care. Maybe it will encourage her to read, you say.

So now it's your feet, your back, and your heart. You can't run, you can't do yoga. You try riding a bike, thinking you'll turn into an Armstrong, but it kills your back. So you stick to walking. You do it one hour each morning and one hour each night. There is no rush to the head, no tearing up your lungs, no massive shock to your system, but it's better than nothing.

A month later the law student leaves you for one of her classmates, tells you that it was great but she has to start being realistic. Translation: I got to stop fucking with old dudes. Later you see her with said classmate on the Yard. He's even lighter than you but he still looks unquestionably black. He's also like nine feet tall and put together like an anatomy primer. They are walking hand in hand and she looks so very happy that you try to find the space in your heart not to begrudge her. Two seconds later, security approaches you and asks for ID. The next day a whitekid on a bike throws a can of Diet Coke at you.

Classes start and by then the squares on your abdomen have

been reabsorbed, like tiny islands in a rising sea of lard. You scan the incoming junior faculty for a possible, but there's nothing. You watch a lot of TV. Sometimes Elvis joins you since his wife doesn't allow him to smoke weed in the house. He's taken up yoga now, having seen what it did for you. Lots of ho's, too, he says, grinning. You want not to hate him.

What happened to the Cape Verdean girl?

What Cape Verdean girl? he says dryly.

You make little advances. You start doing push-ups and pull-ups and even some of your old yoga moves, but very carefully. You have dinner with a couple of girls. One of them is married and hot for days in the late-thirties Dominican middle-class woman sort of way. You can tell she's contemplating sleeping with you and the whole time you're eating your short ribs you feel like you're on the dock. In Santo Domingo I'd never be able to meet you like this, she says with great generosity. Almost all her conversations start with In Santo Domingo. She's doing a year at the business school and for how much she gushes about Boston you can tell she misses the DR, would never live anywhere else.

Boston is really racist, you offer by way of orientation.

She looks at you like you're crazy. Boston isn't racist, she says. She also scoffs at the idea of racism in Santo Domingo.

So Dominicans *love* Haitians now?

That's not about race. She pronounces every syllable. That's about *nationality*.

Of course you end up in bed and it ain't bad except for the fact that she never never comes and she spends a lot of time complaining about her husband. She takes, if you get my meaning, and soon you are squiring her around the city and beyond: to Salem on Halloween and one weekend to the Cape. No one ever pulls you over when you are with her or asks you for ID. Everywhere you two go she shoots fotos but never any of you. She writes her kids postcards while you're in bed.

At the end of the semester she returns home. My home, not your home, she says tetchily. She's always trying to prove you're not Dominican. If I'm not Dominican then no one is, you shoot back, but she laughs at that. Say that in Spanish, she challenges and of course you can't. Last day you drive her to the airport and there is no crushing *Casablanca* kiss, just a smile and a little gay-ass hug and her fake breasts push against you like something irrevocable. Write, you tell her, and she says, Por supuesto, and of course neither of you do. You eventually erase her contact info from your phone but not the pictures you took of her in bed while she was naked and asleep, never those.

Year 4

Wedding invitations from the ex-sucias start to arrive in the mail. You have no idea how to explain this berserkería. What the fuck, you say. You reach out to Arlenny for insight. She turns over the cards. I guess it's what Oates said: Revenge is living well, without you. Fuck Hall and Oates, Elvis says. These bitches think we're bitches. They think we're gonna give a shit about vaina like this. He peers at the invite. Is it me or does every Asian girl on the planet marry a white guy? Is it written on the genes or something?

That year your arms and legs begin to give you trouble, occasionally going numb, flickering in and out like a brownout back on the Island. It is a strange pins-and-needles feeling. What the fuck is this? you wonder. I hope I'm not dying. You're probably working out too hard, Elvis says. But I'm not really working out at all, you protest. Probably just stress, the nurse at emergency care tells you. You hope so, flexing your hands, worrying. You really do hope so.

March you fly out to the Bay to deliver a lecture, which does not go well; almost no one shows up beyond those who were forced to by their professors. Afterward you head alone to K-town and gorge on kalbi until you're ready to burst. You drive around for a couple of hours, just to get a feel of the city. You have a couple of friends in town but you don't call them because you know they'll only want to talk to you about old times, about the ex. You have a sucia in town too and in the end you call her but when she hears your name she hangs up on your ass.

When you return to Boston the law student is waiting for

you in the lobby of your building. You are surprised and excited and a little wary. What's up?

It's like bad television. You notice that she has lined up three suitcases in the foyer. And on closer inspection her ridiculously Persian-looking eyes are red from crying, her mascara freshly applied.

I'm pregnant, she says.

At first you don't register it. You joke: And?

You *asshole*. She starts crying. It's probably your stupid fucking kid.

There are surprises and there are surprises and then there is this.

You don't know what to say or how to act, so you bring her upstairs. You lug up the suitcases despite your back, despite your foot, despite your flickering arms. She says nothing, just hugs her pillow to her Howard sweater. She is a Southern girl with supremely straight posture and when she sits down you feel as if she's preparing to interview you. After serving her tea you ask: Are you keeping it?

Of course I'm keeping *it*.

What about Kimathi?

She doesn't get it. Who?

Your Kenyan. You can't bring yourself to say *boyfriend*.

He threw me out. He knows it's not his. She picks at something on her sweater. I'm going to unpack, OK? You nod and watch her. She is an exceptionally beautiful girl. You think of that old saying *Show me a beautiful girl and I'll show you some-one who is tired of fucking her.* You doubt you would have ever tired of her, though.

But it could be his, right?

It's yours, OK? she cries. I know you don't want it to be yours but it's yours.

You are surprised at how hollowed out you feel. You don't know if you should show enthusiasm or support. You run your hand over the thinning stubble on your head.

I need to stay here, she tells you later, after the two of you fumble through an awkward fuck. I have nowhere to go. I can't go back to my family.

When you tell Elvis the whole story you expect him to flip out, to order you to kick her out. You fear his reaction because you know you don't have the heart to kick her out.

But Elvis doesn't flip. He slaps you on the back, beams delightedly. That's great, cuz.

What do you mean, That's great?

You're going to be a father. You're going to have a son.

A son? What are you talking about? There's not even proof that it's mine.

Elvis is not listening. He's smiling at some inner thought. He checks to make sure the wife is not anywhere in earshot. Remember the last time we went to the DR?

Of course you do. Three years ago. Everybody had a blast except for you. You were in the middle of the great downturn,

which meant you spent most of your time alone, floating on
your back in the ocean or getting drunk at the bar or walking
the beach in the early morning before anybody was up.

What about it?

Well, I got a girl pregnant while we were down there.

Are you fucking kidding me?

He nods.

Pregnant?

He nods again.

Did she have it?

He rummages through his cell phone. Shows you a picture
of a perfect little boy with the most Dominican little face you
ever done saw.

That's my son, Elvis says proudly. Elvis Xavier Junior.

Dude, are you fucking *serious* with this? If your wife finds—

He bridles. She ain't going to find out.

You sit on it for a bit. You're posted up behind his house, near
Central Square. In summer these blocks are ill with activity but
today you can actually hear a jay chivvying some other birds.

Babies are fucking expensive. Elvis punches you in the arm.
So just get ready, buster, to be broke as a joke.

Back at the apartment the law student has taken over two of
your closets and almost your entire sink and most crucially she
has laid claim to the bed. She has put a pillow and a sheet on
the couch. For you.

What, am I not allowed to share the bed with you?

I don't think it's good for me, she says. It would be too stressful. I don't want to miscarry.

Hard to argue against that. Your back doesn't take to the couch at all, so now you wake up in the morning in more pain than ever.

Only a bitch of color comes to Harvard to get pregnant. White women don't do that. Asian women don't do that. Only fucking black and Latina women. Why go to all the trouble to get into Harvard just to get knocked up? You could have stayed on the block and done that shit.

This is what you write in your journal. The next day when you return from classes the law student throws the notebook in your face. I fucking *hate you*, she wails. I *hope* it's not yours. I *hope* it *is* yours and it's born *retarded.*

How can you say that? you demand. How can you say something like that?

She walks to the kitchen and starts to pour herself a shot and you find yourself pulling the bottle out of her hand and pouring its contents into the sink. This is ridiculous, you say. More bad TV.

She doesn't speak to you again for two whole fucking weeks. You spend as much time as you can either at your office or over at Elvis's house. Whenever you enter a room she snaps shut her laptop. I'm not fucking snooping, you say. But she waits for you to move on before she returns to typing whatever she was typing.

You can't throw out your baby's mom, Elvis reminds you. It would fuck that kid up for life. Plus, it's bad karma. Just wait till the baby comes. She'll fucking straighten out.

A month passes, two months pass. You're afraid to tell anybody else, to share the—what? Good news? Arlenny you know would march right in and boot her ass out on the street. Your back is agony and the numbness in your arms is starting to become pretty steady. In the shower, the only place in the apartment you can be alone, you whisper to yourself: *Hell, Netley. We're in Hell.*

LATER IT WILL all come back to you as a terrible fever dream but at the time it moved so very slowly, felt so very concrete. You take her to her appointments. You help her with the vitamins and shit. You pay for almost everything. She is not speaking to her mother so all she has are two friends who are in the apartment almost as much as you are. They are all part of the Biracial Identity Crisis Support Group and look at you with little warmth. You wait for her to melt, but she keeps her distance. Some days while she is sleeping and you are trying to work you allow yourself the indulgence of wondering what kind of child you will have. Whether it will be a boy or a girl, smart or withdrawn. Like you or like her.

Have you thought up any names? Elvis's wife asks.

Not yet.

Taína for a girl, she suggests. And Elvis for a boy. She throws a taunting glance at her husband and laughs.

I like my name, Elvis says. I would give it to a boy.

Over my dead body, his wife says. And besides, this oven is closed for business.

At night while you're trying to sleep you see the glow of her computer through the open door of the bedroom, hear her fingers on the keyboard.

Do you need anything?

I'm fine, thank you.

You come to the door a few times and watch her, wanting to be called in, but she always glares and asks you, What the fuck do you want?

Just checking.

Five month, six month, seventh month. You are in class teaching Intro to Fiction when you get a text from one of her girlfriends saying she has gone into labor, six weeks early. All sorts of terrible fears race around inside of you. You keep trying her cell phone but she doesn't answer. You call Elvis but he doesn't answer either, so you drive over to the hospital by yourself.

Are you the father? the woman at the desk asks.

I am, you say diffidently.

You are led around the corridors and finally given some scrubs and told to wash your hands and given instructions where you should stand and warned about the procedure but as soon as you walk into the birthing room the law student shrieks: *I don't want him in here. I don't want him in here. He's not the father.*

You didn't think anything could hurt so bad. Her two girl-friends rush at you but you have already exited. You saw her thin ashy legs and the doctor's back and little else. You're glad you didn't see anything more. You would have felt like you'd violated her safety or something. You take off the scrubs; you wait around for a bit and then you realize what you're doing and finally you drive home.

YOU DON'T HEAR from her but from her girlfriend, the same one who texted you about the labor. I'll come pick up her bags, OK? When she arrives, she glances around the apartment warily. You're not going to go psycho on me, are you?

No, I'm not. After a pause you demand: Why would you say that? I've never hurt a woman in my life. Then you realize how you sound—like a dude who hurts women all the time. Every-thing goes back into the three suitcases and then you help her wrestle them down to her SUV.

You must be relieved, she says.

You don't answer.

And that's the end of it. Later you hear that the Kenyan visited her in the hospital, and when he saw the baby a teary reconciliation occurred, all was forgiven.

That was your mistake, Elvis said. You should have had a baby with that ex of yours. Then she wouldn't have left you.

She would have left you, Arlenny says. Believe it.

The rest of the semester ends up being a super-duper clusterfuck. Lowest evaluations in your six years as a professor. Your only student of color for that semester writes: He claims that we don't know anything but doesn't show us any way to address these deficiencies. One night you call your ex and when the voice mail clicks on you say: We should have had a kid. And then you hang up, ashamed. Why did you say that? you ask yourself. Now she'll definitely never speak to you again.

I don't think the phone call is the problem, Arlenny says.

Check it out. Elvis produces a picture of Elvis Jr. holding a bat. This kid is going to be a monster.

On winter break you fly to the DR with Elvis. What the hell else are you going to do? You ain't got shit going on, outside of waving your arms around every time they go numb.

Elvis is beyond excited. He has three suitcases of shit for the boy, including his first glove, his first ball, his first Bosox jersey. About eighty kilos of clothes and shit for the baby mama. Hid them all in your apartment, too. You are at his house when he bids his wife and mother-in-law and daughter goodbye. His daughter doesn't seem to understand what's happening but when the door shuts she lets out a wail that coils about you like constantine wire. Elvis stays cool as fuck. This used to be me, you're thinking. Me me me.

Of course you look for her on the flight. You can't help yourself.

You assume that the baby mama will live somewhere poor like Capotillo or Los Alcarrizos but you didn't imagine she would live in the Nadalands. You've been to the Nadalands a couple of times before; shit, your family came up out of those spaces. Squatter chawls where there are no roads, no lights, no running water, no grid, no anything, where everybody's slapdash house is on top of everybody else's, where it's all mud and shanties and motos and grind and thin smiling motherfuckers everywhere without end, like falling off the rim of civilization. You have to leave the rental jípeta on the last bit of paved road and jump on the back of motoconchos with all the luggage balanced on your backs. Nobody stares because those ain't real loads you're carrying: You've seen a single moto carry a family of five and their pig.

You finally pull up to a tiny little house and out comes Baby Mama—cue happy homecoming. You wish you could say you remember Baby Mama from that long-ago trip, but you do not. She is tall and very thick, exactly how Elvis always likes them. She is no older than twenty-one, twenty-two, with an irresistible Georgina Duluc smile, and when she sees you she gives you a huge abrazo. So the padrino finally decides to visit, she declaims in one of those loud ronca campesina voices. You also meet her mother, her grandmother, her brother, her sister, her three uncles. Seems like everybody is missing teeth.

Elvis picks up the boy. Mi hijo, he sings. Mi hijo.

The boy starts crying.

Baby Mama's place is barely two rooms, one bed, one chair, a little table, a single bulb overhead. More mosquitoes than a refugee camp. Raw sewage in the back. You look at Elvis like what the fuck. The few family fotos hanging on the walls are water-stained. When it rains—Baby Mama lifts up her hands —everything goes.

Don't worry, Elvis says, I'm moving them out this month, if I can get the loot together.

The happy couple leaves you with the family and Elvis Jr. while they visit various negocios to settle accounts and to pick up some necessaries. Baby Mama also wants to show off Elvis, natch.

You sit on a plastic chair in front of the house with the kid in your lap. The neighbors admire you with cheerful avidity. A domino game breaks out and you team up with Baby Mama's brooding brother. Takes him less than five seconds to talk you into ordering a couple of grandes and a bottle of Brugal from the nearby colmado. Also three boxes of cigarettes, a tube of salami, and some cough syrup for a neighbor lady with a congested daughter. Ta muy mal, she says. Of course everybody has a sister or a prima they want you to meet. Que tan mas buena que el Diablo, they guarantee. You all barely finish the first bottle of romo before some of the sisters and primas actually start coming around. They look rough but you got to give it to them for trying. You invite them all to sit down, order more beer and some bad pica pollo.

Just let me know which one you like, a neighbor whispers, and I'll make it happen.

Elvis Jr. watches you with considerable gravitas. He is a piercingly cute carajito. He has all these mosquito bites on his legs and an old scab on his head no one can explain to you. You are suddenly overcome with the urge to cover him with your arms, with your whole body.

Later, Elvis Sr. fills you in on the Plan. I'll bring him over to the States in a few years. I'll tell the wife he was an accident, a one-time thing when I was drunk and I didn't find out about it until now.

And that's going to work?

It will work out, he says testily.

Bro, your wife ain't going to buy that.

And what the fuck do you know? Elvis says. It ain't like your shit ever works.

Can't argue with that. By this point your arms are killing you so you pick up the boy in order to put circulation back in them. You look into his eyes. He looks into yours. He seems preternaturally sapient. MIT-bound, you say, while you nuzzle his peppercorn hair. He starts to bawl then and you put him down, watch him run around a while.

That's more or less when you know.

The second story of the house is unfinished, rebar poking

out of the cinderblock like horrible gnarled follicles, and you and Elvis stand up there and drink beers and stare out beyond the edge of the city, beyond the vast radio dish antennas in the distance, out toward the mountains of the Cibao, the Cordillera Central, where your father was born and where your ex's whole family is from. It's breathtaking.

He's not yours, you tell Elvis.

What are you talking about?

The boy is not yours.

Don't be a jerk. That kid looks just like me.

Elvis. You put your hand on his arm. You look straight into the center of his eyes. Cut the crap.

A long silence. But he looks like me.

Bro, he so doesn't look like you.

The next day you two load up the boy and drive back into the city, back into Gazcue. You literally have to beat the family off to keep them from coming with you. Before you go one of the uncles pulls you aside. You really should bring these people a refrigerator. Then the brother pulls you aside. And a TV. And then the mother pulls you aside. A hot comb too.

Traffic back into the center is Gaza Strip crazy and there seems to be a crash every five hundred meters and Elvis keeps threatening to turn around. You ignore him. You stare at the slurry of broken concrete, the sellers with all the crap of the earth slung over their shoulders, the dust-covered palms.

The boy holds on to you tightly. There is no significance in this, you tell yourself. It's a Moro-type reflex, nothing more.

Don't make me do this, Yunior, Elvis pleads.

You insist. You have to, E. You know you can't live a lie. It won't be good for the boy, it won't be good for you. Don't you think it's better to know?

But I always wanted a boy, he says. My whole life that's all I wanted. When I got in that shit in Iraq I kept thinking, Please God let me live just long enough to have a son, please, and then you can kill me dead right after. And look, He gave him to me, didn't He? He gave him to me.

The clinic is in one of those houses they built in the International Style during the time of Trujillo. The two of you stand at the front desk. You are holding the boy's hand. The boy is staring at you with lapidary intensity. The mud is waiting. The mosquito bites are waiting. The Nada is waiting.

Go on, you tell Elvis.

In all honesty you figure he won't do it, that this is where it will end. He'll take the boy and turn around and go back to the jípeta. But he carries the little guy into a room where they swab both their mouths and it's done.

You ask: How long will it take for the results?

Four weeks, the technician tells you.

That long?

She shrugs. Welcome to Santo Domingo.

Year 5

You figure that's the last you'll hear about it, that no matter what, the results will change nothing. But four weeks after the trip, Elvis informs you that the test is negative. Fuck, he says bitterly, fuck fuck fuck. And then he cuts off all contact with the kid and the mother. Changes his cell phone number and e-mail account. I told the bitch not to call me again. There is some shit that can't be forgiven.

Of course you feel terrible. You think about the way the boy looked at you. Let me have her number at least, you say. You figure you can throw her a little cash every month but he won't have it. Fuck that lying bitch.

You reckon he must have known, somewhere inside, maybe even wanted you to blow it all up, but you let it be, don't explore it. He's going to yoga five times a week now, is in the best shape of his life, while you on the other hand have to buy bigger jeans again. When you walk into Elvis's now, his daughter rushes you, calls you Tío Junji. It's your Korean name, Elvis teases.

With him it's like nothing happened. You wish you could be as phlegmatic.

Do you ever think about them?

He shakes his head. Never will either.

The numbness in the arms and legs increases. You return to

your doctors and they ship you over to a neurologist who sends you out for an MRI. Looks like you have stenosis all down your spine, the doctor reports, impressed.

Is it bad?

It isn't great. Did you used to do a lot of heavy manual labor?

Besides delivering pool tables, you mean?

That would do it. The doctor squints at the MRI. Let's try some physical therapy. If that doesn't work we'll talk about other options.

Like?

He steeples his fingers contemplatively. Surgery.

From there what little life you got goes south. A student complains to the school that you curse too much. You have to have a sit-down with the dean, who more or less tells you to watch your shit. You get pulled over by the cops three weekends in a row. One time they sit you out on the curb and you watch as all the other whips sail past, passengers ogling you as they go. On the T you swear you peep her in the rush-hour mix and for a second your knees buckle but it turns out to be just another Latina mujerón in a tailored suit.

Of course you dream about her. You are in New Zealand or in Santo Domingo or improbably back in college, in the dorms. You want her to say your name, to touch you, but she doesn't. She just shakes her head.

Ya.

You want to move on, to exorcise shit, so you find a new apartment on the other side of the square that has a view of Harvard skyline. All those amazing steeples, including your favorite, the gray dagger of the Old Cambridge Baptist Church. In the first days of your tenancy an eagle lands in the dead tree right outside your fifth-story window. Looks you in the eye. This seems to you like a good sign.

A month later the law student sends you an invitation to her wedding in Kenya. There's a foto and the two of them are dressed in what you assume is traditional Kenyan jumpoffs. She looks very thin, and she's wearing a lot of makeup. You expect a note, some mention of what you did for her, but there is nothing. Even the address was typed on a computer.

Maybe it's a mistake, you say.

It wasn't a mistake, Arlenny assures you.

Elvis tears the invite up, throws it out the truck window. Fuck that bitch. Fuck all bitches.

You manage to save a tiny piece of the foto. It's of her hand.

You work harder than you've ever worked at everything— the teaching, your physical therapy, your regular therapy, your reading, your walking. You keep waiting for the heaviness to leave you. You keep waiting for the moment you never think about the ex again. It doesn't come.

You ask everybody you know: How long does it usually take to get over it?

There are many formulas. One year for every year you dated. Two years for every year you dated. It's just a matter of will-power: The day you decide it's over, it's over. You never get over it.

One night that winter you go out with all the boys to a ghetto-ass Latin club in Mattapan Square. Murder-fucking-pan. Outside it's close to zero, but inside it's so hot that every-body's stripped down to their T-shirts and the funk is as thick as a fro. There's a girl who keeps bumping into you. You say to her Pero mi amor, ya. And she says: Ya yourself. She's Domin-ican and lithe and super tall. I could never date anyone as short as you, she informs you very early on in your conversations. But she gives you her number at the end of the night. All even-ing, Elvis sits at the bar quietly, drinking shot after shot of Rémy. The week before, he took a quick solo trip to the DR, a ghost recon. Didn't tell you about it until after. He tried look-ing for the mom and Elvis Jr. but they had moved and no one knew where they were. None of the numbers he had for her worked. I hope they turn up, he says.

I hope so, too.

You take the longest walks. Every ten minutes you drop and do squats or push-ups. It's not running, but it raises your heart rate, better than nothing. Afterward you are in so much nerve pain that you can barely move.

Some nights you have *Neuromancer* dreams where you see the ex and the boy and another figure, familiar, waving at you in the distance. *Somewhere, very close, the laugh that wasn't laughter.*

And finally, when you feel like you can do so without blowing into burning atoms, you open a folder you have kept hidden under your bed. The Doomsday Book. Copies of all the e-mails and fotos from the cheating days, the ones the ex found and compiled and mailed to you a month after she ended it. *Dear Yunior, for your next book.* Probably the last time she wrote your name.

You read the whole thing cover to cover (yes, she put covers on it). You are surprised at what a fucking chickenshit coward you are. It kills you to admit it but it's true. You are astounded by the depths of your mendacity. When you finish the Book a second time you say the truth: You did the right thing, negra. You did the right thing.

She's right; this would make a killer book, Elvis says. The two of you have been pulled over by a cop and are waiting for Officer Dickhead to finish running your license. Elvis holds up one of the fotos.

She's Colombian, you say.

He whistles. Que viva Colombia. Hands you back the Book. You really should write the cheater's guide to love.

You think?

I do.

It takes a while. You see the tall girl. You go to more doctors. You celebrate Arlenny's Ph.D. defense. And then one June night you scribble the ex's name and: *The half-life of love is forever.*

You bust out a couple more things. Then you put your head down.

The next day you look at the new pages. For once you don't want to burn them or give up writing forever.

It's a start, you say to the room.

That's about it. In the months that follow you bend to the work, because it feels like hope, like grace—and because you know in your lying cheater's heart that sometimes a start is all we ever get.